Hide the Baron

His mouth was ⬛⬛⬛
were trying to conve⬛⬛⬛
*sound, just a husky whisper which did not make
sense, coming from the back of his throat. . . .*

*"Jimmy," she said, quite steadily now, "don't
talk, or you'll make it worse."*

He ignored her.

*She slid a pillow out of a slip, folded the slip,
and pressed it gently on the wound, where the blood
was slowly pulsing out. He was moving his right
hand, towards the corner, much as Gedde had done.*

"Jimmy, lie still!"

*Suddenly, alarmingly, his voice became
strong. That was so unexpected that she stopped
what she was doing.*

*"Take the miniatures and take them to Man-
nering," he said. "They're in the seat of my chair.
Tell no one, y'understand? No one. Take them to
John Man——"*

*He stopped, and his voice faded as suddenly
as it had strengthened. He grabbed her hand. She
sensed his fear, and shared it. His eyes were very
bright and rounded, he looked at her as if pleadingly.*

"Jimmy!" she breathed.

*Then his eyes closed, as if putting out a light,
and his frail body sagged. After a second the tightness of his grip on her arm slackened.*

"Jimmy," she breathed again.

There were tears in her eyes.

Other titles in the Walker British Mystery Series

HIDE THE BARON

John Creasey

as Anthony Morton

WALKER AND COMPANY · NEW YORK

First published in the United States of America in 1978 by the
Walker Publishing Company, Inc.

This paperback edition first published in 1985.

ISBN: 0-8027-3131-7

Library of Congress Catalog Card Number 77-91362

Printed in the United States of America

10   9   8   7   6   5   4   3   2

This edition printed in 1986.

CONTENTS

1

THE TRAP

JOANNA CAUGHT SIGHT OF GEORGE MERROW AMONG THE trees, and hesitated. The beauty of the evening suddenly lost its quiet and its delight. Until the moment she had seen him, she had been wholly absorbed in the copse through which she was walking, the flitting birds who would soon settle for the night, the tiny, lullaby sounds of the country. Beneath the branches of the pine trees, which grew here with larch and a few oak and beech, she could see the last of the evening sunlight brushing the green of meadows with its gold.

Just beyond the brow of the nearer meadow lay Brook House ; home, as far as she had a home.

That was a sobering thought.

She liked the huge house, she liked and was amused by old Jimmy Garfield, she was ready to love the district. The one worrying factor was George Merrow, and there he stood, lurking among the trees.

Lurking ?

She couldn't see him now. Either he had slipped behind the shadow of larger trees, or, in walking, she had changed the angle at which she had been looking. After the moment's hesitation she walked briskly along the well-defined path. Whatever else, it would be folly to allow Merrow to know how much he worried her.

He could not be more than fifty yards away.

Looking out for him, and yet pretending that she had not noticed that anyone was there, made her oblivious of all the other things that went on around her. She did not know that his were not the only pair of eyes watching. She quickened her pace, looked intently ahead along the path. She had once been told that when she walked like that, with long easy stride, shoulders back

and arms swinging, she put men in mind of the Goddess
Diana. She wasn't thinking about that then, but here
she was among the trees, where a huntress might find a
target, quite unaware of the fact that she looked boldly
handsome ; enough to make even timid men stop to stare.
The old green tweed skirt, the rust-coloured linen blouse
with its shallow V, the way her brown hair was coiled
about her head, were all part of the vivid picture.

She didn't see Merrow.

Perhaps she'd misjudged him ; perhaps he'd gone on.

She reached the densest part of the little copse, where
the thicket was badly overgrown and where, the previous
evening, she had seen a family of field-mice playing.
None was there now.

It was dark in the thicket, and the distant brightness
was hidden.

Well, she could deal with a difficult man, couldn't she ?
She had to deal with this one ; sooner or later the ' affair '
would have to come to a head. The odd, ironic fact
was that if Merrow had not been so aggressive, as if he
took it for granted that his looks would make all conquests easy, she would not have disliked him. His looks,
carriage, clothes and general manner were all very much
in his favour. She knew little about him, except that
he was a nephew of Jimmy Garfield, and that he had
travelled a great deal. Once, talking to them after
dinner, he'd held even the old man's attention closely
with a story of a journey through India. Odd comments,
none boastful, betrayed his familiarity with the Near
East, the Far East, and even parts of South America.

He was still out of sight.

Perhaps he had chosen to go ahead on the short cut
which she knew he used whenever he was alone. It
meant crossing the stream, which wasn't easy for her ;
she'd only tried it once, and split the seam of her skirt.

Among George Merrow's undoubted virtues was physical
strength and agility ; he could jump that stream from a
standing start, with no effort at all.

Either he was out of sight, or else actually waiting for

her ; surely the only word to describe that was ' lurking '. She strode along, wishing that she weren't so obsessed with thought of Merrow, hoping that she wasn't flushing. She flushed too easily, often for the silliest of reasons.

If he weren't behind the next oak tree, which had stood there for three hundred years and——

He was.

He stepped out in front of her, so swiftly that it made her heart leap wildly. He timed the move to perfection, and she couldn't avoid him, desperately though she tried. In a moment his arms were round her, he held her tightly, and before she could strain away from him, kissed her full and lingeringly on the lips. Then he moved one arm, held her chin firmly, and kissed her again ; and then, still with one arm round her waist, he eased away, and looked into her eyes.

" The colour of honey," he said very softly. " *That* is what I think of you, Joanna." He kissed her again.

She hadn't attempted to struggle, had just held herself stiff. She felt the tightness of his arm relax, until she was free to move away. She moved, as swiftly as he had done, and he looked startled. Before he could speak, even before the surprise had faded, she struck the side of his face with the flat of her hand ; every ounce of her strength was in the blow. It made him lose his balance and bump against the rugged trunk of the centuries' old oak.

He stayed there, looking bewildered ; baffled.

" *That*," she said, " is what I think of you."

She stalked past him.

She had an uneasy, scared kind of feeling that he would follow, and that she might have made him desperately angry. She also had a feeling, it was no stronger, that fires few people suspected burnt deep in George Merrow. There was something of the primitive about him ; his cave-man tactics were natural to him.

The truth was, he frightened her.

Her heart thudded, she wanted to hurry so that she could reach the meadow, where movement was freer, but she made herself walk, and wouldn't look round. She heard nothing. The soft grass of the meadow was only a few yards away now ; she was in the fringe of the trees ; she could see the castellated top of Brook House.

There was no sound of Merrow following her.

She looked round, and he wasn't in sight. That brought a relief from tension, but she didn't slacken her pace. Now that the crisis was past, she coloured furiously and uncontrollably ; her cheeks stung as if they were burning. She felt first hot, then cold, as the evening's breeze blew down from the top of the hill.

The copse lay behind her and to her right, very thick in the direction in which George Merrow had gone. She could not hear him walking. She could not imagine what he looked like, or what he was feeling. The one certain thing was that she couldn't stay in this job if this was the way things were to go. In fact it would be wiser to leave, this week-end ; easier to get the parting over quickly. She had come on a month's trial and could tell Jimmy that she just wasn't contented, the country-side was too lonely for her. That way she wouldn't have to tell the truth ; and the truth would probably worry the old man, who had a noticeably soft spot for his nephew.

She didn't want to leave. It wasn't everyone's job, but she liked it. 'Secretary' was the word used to describe the dozen and one jobs she had to do, and she was in fact a secretary in that she wrote letters and attended generally to correspondence. For the rest, the work was greatly varied, from driving Jimmy about if he felt like a run in his Rolls-Royce, to taking his Ovaltine to him last thing at night.

"You really want a chauffeur-valet," she'd said to him, only two nights ago.

"Don't want anything of the kind," he'd answered in his hoarse cracked voice. "Want just what I've got—a handsome young woman dancing attendance on me ! Think a man's eye is any different because he's a septuagenarian ? "

She'd laughed ; something about him made it easy to laugh, even when he said conventionally outrageous things.

He would be sorry to lose her, and she would be sorry to go ; but the situation developing with George Merrow was inescapable. Even if George relaxed his pressure for a little while, it was probable that he would break out again at any time. Oh, admit it, the best thing to do about an unpleasant situation was to change it before it became worse. She could get another job, if not such a good one, and——

She was fifty yards from the edge of the copse, walking more slowly because the meadow sloped upwards, when she heard the screech. It made her stop quite still, and listen. It came again, a yelp more than a screech this time, and seemed to tell of acute pain.

It came a third time, and began to scare her.

Then it settled down to a high-pitched whining, but the shrillness of the first yelps had gone right through Joanna, and she felt shivery. Now she stood still, looking towards the sound. It didn't quieten, and was as if a dog were in pain. She listened, half expecting to hear Merrow call out to reassure it, or even talk to it, because voices travelled far and clearly ; that sound, little more than whimpering, seemed close at hand.

If Merrow had gone striding on, beyond the stream, he might not have heard. . . .

She heard a different sound ; a metallic kind of noise, harsh and grating, with a hint of clanging about it ; and as it came, a gasp and a single, short, sharp word. The whimpering stopped ; so did the other sounds. Fifty yards of meadow land and perhaps twenty yards of the copse hid her from whatever was happening, but she didn't go towards the noises, just stood staring, as if willing herself the power to see through trees.

Then :

" *Joanna*," George Merrow called, in a clear, controlled voice.

She didn't call back, and still didn't move. His voice seemed to echo, clear but empty of expression.

The dog whimpered.

" If you can hear, please come at once," Merrow called very deliberately.

It might be a trap.

She snapped her fingers at herself, then began to hurry towards the spot. Once on the move, she couldn't move fast enough. ' Trap ' be hanged, she was thinking in terms of silly melodrama ; that was the way he affected her. Something really strange had happened, had driven the half sneer out of his voice.

She called : " Coming ! Keep calling out, I'll know where you are."

" Thanks. Head for the rhododendrons."

" All right."

There was only a small clump of rhododendrons near, and as Joanna made for it, she reflected that Merrow knew the whole of the grounds thoroughly ; almost as if he had lived here for years, instead of a few months.

The whimpering of the dog persuaded her that there was really grave trouble, that both of them needed help urgently.

" Keep to the right of the clump," he called, in a normal speaking voice, " and watch the ground carefully."

" Why ? "

" Traps."

" What ? "

He chuckled, and for a perverse reason that annoyed her. A few nights ago the subject after dinner had turned to cruelty to animals, blood sports and traps. Jimmy Garfield took a strong line : all blood sports and all forms of traps were cruelty, according to the old man ; but Merrow had defended blood sports, and even praised them—yet in a way which hadn't riled the old man.

Joanna watched the ground, here thick grass, there leaf-mould, and saw nothing remotely like a trap. She avoided any spot where one might be hidden by the autumn's thick growth of fern and bramble. Blackberries, tight and red and giving no sign of coming black lusciousness, were very thick.

" Turn left at the path," Merrow called.

He sounded very near.

The dog whimpered only occasionally. Further away there was the sound of running water, at the tiny waterfall in the middle of the copse. A match scraped ; as if Merrow was lighting a cigarette.

Joanna reached the well-trod path, went right, and then found the spot where he turned towards the stream. She saw him on one knee, a cigarette at his lips, looking stark white against his tanned face. It was gloomy in here ; only in the distance did the evening light seem bright.

His leg was caught just above the ankle. The trap was big, black and ugly looking, and she could see the claws on either side of his leg. And it had closed on him with vicious strength—was holding the leg in a vice, was probably touching the bone. He must be suffering agony, but he knelt there, looking at her with a funny kind of grin.

" Nice of you to forgive," he said. " Thanks. It's been tampered with. I can't unspring it. I'm all right for a minute, go and see how the dog is, will you ? I can't see him, but he's not far along."

" Never mind the dog. You——"

" This is one time when we're not going to argue," Merrow said crisply. Now that she was closer, she could see the sweat on his forehead and his upper lip, and he couldn't keep the look of pain out of his eyes ; his lips were set, too, between the words. He was gripping a small tree tightly with his left hand.

" You're a fool," she said tartly.

But she hurried past him.

The dog was only ten yards away, a liver and white mongrel of terrier size, trapped by the hind paw, turning round and trying to see what was holding him and causing such pain. He heard her, looked up, and yelped.

" Careful with him," Merrow called. " He might bite if he's still in severe pain. Much damage ? "

" It—it looks like—like yours."

" Is he tugging to get free ? "

" No."

" Sensible chap. Joanna, I don't think you'll be able to force the traps open. Will you run hell for leather to the house, and get Gedde ? Then——"

" Of course I can get them open," she said snappishly, " and I'm going to do you first." She hesitated, looking into the dog's pleading eyes. " Lie still," she urged, " don't move, I'll be back in a moment."

She turned her back on the dog.

It yelped, and she knew that it had tried to follow her, and dragged on that injured leg.

" Experiment on the dog," called Merrow, and in spite of the agony he must be in there was a note of mockery in his voice. " Only don't take too long."

2

THE MISSION

SHE WAS ON HER KNEES, BY MERROW'S SIDE, PULLING at the teeth of the trap with all her strength. She felt the perspiration at her forehead; all over her body. She set her teeth. Merrow's handkerchief, folded into a pad, and his leather tobacco pouch, saved her hands from the trap's sharp teeth, but they still hurt.

The dog lay near, watching, not whimpering. It had been easy—well, easier—to open the trap wide enough for the small leg, but this was a different task. She had to look at Merrow's leg, too; the blood smearing his brightly polished shoe and the end of his grey flannel trousers. He was tugging on the other side, and grunting in a curious way which made her look up.

He was staring down at the steel teeth. He'd lost his colour, and had become a dirty grey. Sweat poured down his cheeks. All these things were guides to the pain he was in, and Joanna knew that he couldn't keep on much longer.

Joanna had put a piece of wood between the teeth, as a wedge; they couldn't close so tightly again, but if either of them let go now, they'd snap, and——

" Hold it a second," she pleaded. " Hold on." She took one hand away and the steel closed in slightly. He grunted again. She shifted the wedge further into the corner and stretched for another, thicker one; got it, then put it in; and now she knew that the jaws couldn't close more tightly.

" All right," she said. " You can relax."

He didn't speak, just stopped straining at the trap. If it closed at all, it was only the fraction of an inch. He drooped, badly. She hadn't time to study him, but levered with the stick, which was weathered and tough and didn't splinter or break. Soon, it was close by his ankle, and it was nearly as thick as the ankle itself.

She said : " Now I'm going to take your shoe off, and you can draw your foot through."

He didn't answer.

She unfastened the lace, made it as loose as she could, and drew the shoe off with great gentleness. Her hands were sticky, but she hardly realised that ; or what made them so.

" Now take your foot out," she ordered.

Merrow didn't answer, or move. She looked up, sharply. His eyes were closed and his colour was dreadful ; as of a dying man. His left hand clutched the sapling, and only that kept him up.

" All right," she said. " Just keep still."

She held his leg a little above the ankle and drew it up slowly and with great care, until it was free of the trap. She knew that he had lost consciousness by then. She eased his hand from the sapling, and laid him down, the injured leg bent a little at the knee. Then she stood up, spared a glance for the dog and said : " Wait here, don't try to move." Soon, cold where the wind of her movement struck her, she began to hurry along the path which Merrow had always used, towards the running stream, the leap, and the short cut to the house. This way it wouldn't take more than ten minutes ; well, less than a quarter of an hour. Once she was over the stream and up the hill on the far side, it would be easy going.

She began to run. . . .

The doctor, both youngish and donnish, watched the ambulance men push the stretcher into the ambulance, and then turned to Joanna. He smiled easily if shyly, as if he was also impressed.

" He'll be all right, Miss Woburn, I'm quite sure of that. Nasty laceration and a fracture, but I should think it's clean. We'll have him up and about again in a week or two, and we'll make sure he doesn't suffer too much pain—he's had plenty already."

Joanna nodded.

"I'll take the dog to a vet, too. And I'll have to report this to the police," the doctor added. "It's an offence to put steel traps, any kind of trap for that matter, without authorisation. That type of trap's been illegal in this country for a quarter of a century, too. You may find that the police will come out to see you this evening."

"I can only tell them what I know," Joanna said.

"Just wanted to warn you." The doctor gave a boyish smile. "All right, I'll get off then. Good-night." He shook hands.

Joanna stood in the fading light, on the parkland near the house, and watched first the ambulance and then the doctor's car moving cautiously over the uneven grassland towards the long drive. The ambulance put on its head-lamps, which showed up quite brightly. Behind her the lights were on at the house, most of the windows were glowing ; Jimmy Garfield liked to have brightness about him.

He would be waiting for a report.

Joanna turned and hurried across the parkland, seeing Gedde, the butler and general factotum, going ahead of her ; Gedde always kept his distance, was the aloof, impersonal servant, proper, efficient and civil if not particularly friendly. He seemed to get larger as he drew nearer the radius of the light from the house. He reached the top of the steps, and waited. She hurried up, but at the top couldn't resist turning to look back at the ambulance and the car.

Only the headlights, nearly a mile away, showed at the foot of the drive ; they turned right, towards the town of Orme, and seemed to be going too fast.

Then she went towards the house.

"Mr. Garfield would like to see you, miss," Gedde told her ; as if she didn't know.

"Yes, Gedde, thank you."

"He's in the library, miss."

He was always in the library.

"Thank you, Gedde."

The great hall was skilfully lighted ; only the one big chandelier was visible, the other lighting was concealed, and yet shone upon the great paintings, the tapestries, the sheen of the polished armour and the panelled walls so that everything looked as well as it could.   When she had first stepped inside here she had thought ' baronial ', and nothing had made her change her opinion.   She didn't yet know the history of Brook House, but it was a long one ;   there were seven-foot walls in one part, and two rooms which had been untouched for nearly four hundred years.

The library was on the ground floor, next to the dining-room.   On the other side of it was Garfield's bedroom and bath-room ;   next to that, Gedde's room.   Garfield and Gedde, G. & G.   The floor of the hall was stone-flagged and covered with beautiful skin rugs ;   the floor of the passage was bare and looked as if it ought to be covered with rushes, or with bales of straw, and as if oil flares or flares of pig's grease should be stuck in the iron torch-holders bolted to the stone walls.

She wondered why Garfield had bought this house ; he had been over sixty, she knew, when he had.

Well, a millionaire had every right to do what he liked with his money.

Now that George Merrow was no longer in pain, and in the right hands, Joanna felt an almost guilty feeling of relief.   She would not be forced to take any hasty decision, and it was possible that when Merrow came back his mood would be different.   At least, there would be no issue to face for four or five weeks.

She reached the library door, and knocked.

The knocker was of iron, the shape of a gargoyle, and it rapped against an iron plate.   Jimmy Garfield insisted that everyone should knock before coming in, and she wasn't quite sure why ;   unless he was afraid of being indecorous.   The rule applied to everyone except Gedde, and in the month that Joanna had been here she had learned to take it for granted.

There was no answering call.

She knocked again.

At last she heard him say: "Come in." His voice sounded weak, but occasionally it was, especially if he was very tired, and he would probably be tired after the shock of what had happened. She hadn't seen him yet; all the messages had been relayed by Gedde.

She went in.

She didn't go far, but stood for a moment with a hand at the door handle.

Garfield sat in his wheel-chair, one so beautifully made that it could turn on a sixpence and be moved at a finger-tip touch of the wheels. He was looking at her. White hair crowned him; here was an Old Testament prophet come back to life. Usually he had beautifully clear skin and a ruddy complexion, as if a second childhood were coming in real earnest. His eyes were so bright a blue, too.

Usually, but not now. They were lack-lustre. He looked as if he had received a nasty shock. She knew little about the condition of his heart, except that it was not strong, and he had never discussed his health with her; but now she realised she was looking at a sick man, as distinct from an old man with a spinal condition which made it impossible for him to stand up unaided.

She closed the door and went right into the high room, with its bookcases and desk, its maps, its huge globe, its priceless treasures. Here were a few of the beautiful things he had collected, and which he loved. His collection of bizarre *objets d'art* was world famous, and twice while she had been here he had sent for some of the pieces from his strong-room, and returned others. Now there was a sedate group of African bronzes in a glass case, and in a corner cupboard some beautiful beaten-gold models of pagodas from Siam.

"Hallo, Joanna," he said. "Bring up a chair, and sit down." He blinked, and it was easy to believe that he was trying to throw off the sickness. He actually squared his shoulders. "That's right. Comfortable? Like a drink?"

"No, I——"

"Nonsense. Do you good. Look worn out," Garfield added, and with a touch of the wheel of the chair, turned himself round so that he could stretch out for bottles from a small cocktail cabinet near him; whatever he could do for himself he would do. "Brandy's what you want, too; must have been a nasty shock."

"It wasn't very pleasant."

"Couldn't have been." His voice gradually grew stronger. His hands looked strong, and the bottle shook only a little, the glass hardly at all. Brandy gurgled. "There y'are. Feel better after that." He poured himself out a tiny tot of whisky, and squirted a lot of soda. "Got him free yourself, Gedde says."

"I had to."

"Had to? Ought to've fainted!" He grinned, and although it wasn't the mock-fierce grin she was used to, the one intended to scare the wits out of anyone who saw it for the first time, it showed that he was feeling better. "Drink up, now." They sipped. "I'll find the scoundrel who put those traps there if I have to scour the whole county for him. That's the first thing I want you to do, telephone the police. Not the station, the Superintendent's home. Aylmer's the name. He'll make sure they get a move on. Understand?"

"The doctor said that he'd tell the police," objected Joanna.

"Well, let him! *I* want to tell the Superintendent in person." There was less than his customary vigour in the way Garfield said that. "Well? Feel better?"

"Yes, thanks."

"Early dinner, early bed, that's my prescription for you for the night," he said. "Especially as I've a job for you tomorrow. Important. *Very* important. George was going to do it."

She didn't make any comment. The brandy warmed her and the fumes cleared her head. She felt relaxed, but not as exhausted or as affected as she had expected. It was pleasantly warm in here, and when you were with someone whom you knew liked you, it was a help.

" Was he ? "

" Yes. It's important that someone does it tomorrow, and there aren't many people I can trust. Can't spare Gedde." He often talked about not being able to trust people, and it didn't mean a great deal to Joanna then. " Be ready to go ? "

" Of course."

" That's good," Jimmy Garfield said. " Y'know, Joanna, you're a comfort to an old man. Didn't ever think I'd be able to count myself so lucky. Nice to look at, sensible, competent—hm, yes, well." He really was much better than he had been, and there was a glint in his eyes, which looked clearer and a brighter blue. " How d'you get on with George ? "

He'd never asked her before, and the question took her completely by surprise. She didn't answer. She knew, from the way he looked at her, that her expression had answered for her. He scowled, but a hint of laughter lurked in his eyes ; that was one of the magnificent things about this old man : the fact that he could summon laughter so easily.

" Not surprised," he said. " He's been trying to add to his conquests. Conceited young fool. Every man has his weakness, Joanna ; women were always George's weakness, but with the right woman—never mind. What d'you do, slap his face ? "

She was surprised into a little gust of laughter.

" That's right, you look after yourself if you can. If he gets too fresh, tell me. I'll deal with him ! Rather the two of you worked it out between you, though, never so effective when gentlemanly behaviour is imposed, is it ? " He chuckled. " But don't stand any of his nonsense, Joanna, I'd be on your side." He took a swig of his watered whisky. " Ah. Going to have a stronger nip, damn what the doctors say. You've done me good. You always do me good. Felt like the very devil when you came in. Ever have bad moods ? Ever brood on the past ? Ever been tormented by a *conscience* ? "

He flung that out.

She said : " Well——"

" 'Course you haven't, only an old fool would have asked. Take my advice, Joanna, never do anything that will weigh on your conscience. Twenty years or so ago I did something, and goddam it, the weight gets heavier every year." He stopped, and the brightness faded from his eyes, he was back almost where he had been when she had entered. It was a long time before he perked up, and then it was only with a brief spurt.

" Getting maudlin," he said abruptly. " Never take any notice of an old man. Well, not too much notice." He forced a grin. " All right, Joanna, go and telephone the police but if anyone wants to see me, I'm indisposed. Or tell them the simple truth, eh, don't want to see them, don't intend to see them, and if a septuagenarian millionaire can't see whom the hell he likes, what's the use of age or money ? Eh ? "

She tried to laugh.

" Off with you," he said, and waved her to the door.

She went out, closing the door quietly. In some ways it had been a puzzling twenty minutes, but he often behaved like that, jumping from one subject to another, and apparently obsessed by his age. She wished she knew what had weighed him down so heavily.

No one was in the hall.

It had lost the eeriness that its size and the medieval style had created when she had first come. The stone steps were carpeted, too, and she made no sound going up them. She made little as she went to her room, which was above Jimmy Garfield's, and it wasn't surprising that the maid who was turning down her bed and the housekeeper who was with her had heard nothing.

The maid was saying : " And if you ask me, someone put them there on purpose. Meant to cripple him, that's what I say."

Joanna stopped, abruptly, and stifled an exclamation. Then she waited for what seemed an age, hanging on to the housekeeper's words, as if it mattered whether the older woman agreed or not.

3

THE POLICE

"DON'T TALK SO SOFT," MRS. BADDELOW SAID, "ALL you girls can think of these days is something daft. Make sure there's ice in that drinking water jug, and don't let me hear any more of your nonsense." She turned, saw Joanna, and took that in her stride. "Did you ever hear the like, Miss Woburn? A poacher puts down a few traps, just as poachers have been doing to my knowledge for the last thirty years, and this flibbertigibbet talks about it being put there on purpose. Who'd want to hurt Mr. Merrow?"

The maid said waspishly: "Well, someone wants to hurt him all right. They nearly killed him *last* night."

As the words came out, she began to falter, and lose colour. It was obvious to both Joanna and Mrs. Baddelow that she wished she hadn't spoken. She moistened her lips, and turned, flouncing, towards the bedside table and the vacuum jug fastened by a bracket to the wall.

Mrs. Baddelow stretched an arm across Joanna's bed.

"Oh, no, you don't, young lady! Tell us just what you mean by that."

She was tall and thin and angular, and could beat a carpet or wring a blanket with the best. Now, she seized the girl's arm, and made her turn round. It was as if she saw this as a trial of strength which she dared not lose.

"Out with it, now."

"Don't, you're hurting."

"You'll know what getting hurt means, if I have to give a bad report to your pa," said Mrs. Baddelow ominously; but she let the girl's arm go. "You soft thing, I'm here to help you, not to scare the life out of

23

you. So's Miss Woburn. Now let's know what happened, Prissy, and don't have any half-truths."

The maid, Priscilla, stood there and rubbed her wrist. She still looked scared, and Mrs. Baddelow's matter-of-factness threw that into sharp relief. She was a fair-haired, attractive little creature, with curves which she flattened down when on duty, but exaggerated when she was out; when out, she also made up recklessly and adopted a walk which was doubtless meant to be like Marilyn Monroe's. She had fluffy fair hair, a nice skin and eyes as blue as Jimmy Garfield's.

Mrs. Baddelow rounded the bed.

" Now what is it, Priscilla ? " She didn't take the girl's wrist again, but stood very close. " What's this talk about Mr. Merrow nearly being killed ? Either it's the truth or a lie. If it's true we need to know more about it, and if it's a lie—well, we'll come to that later."

" It isn't a lie ! "

" How did you come to be in possession of such remarkable truths, then ? " asked Mrs. Baddelow. One had to add plainness to her angularity, and a voice which had something of the harshness of a crow's; but obviously she meant to get at the truth.

Joanna was feeling less agitated, yet somehow she knew that whatever Priscilla had to say affected her much more than it should.

" Come *on*," Mrs. Baddelow urged.

" Oh, all right," Priscilla said, " someone shot at him."

She stood a little way from the housekeeper, eyes bright with defiance, nice lips unsteady. Yet she would hardly be scared, now, of something which she believed had happened the previous night. Would she ?

Mrs. Baddelow's voice and manner told of both scepticism and scorn.

" And how do *you* know, pray ? "

Priscilla didn't answer, just turned a flaming red.

Suddenly, Joanna seemed to know part of the answer, and it affected her in a painful, disturbing way. She wanted to send the two women away, without hearing anything more ; she felt quite sure what the girl would say next, and didn't want to hear it.

She didn't want to hear it.

She would have to.

Mrs. Baddelow seemed to have made some kind of guess, too, and it affected her manner. She looked worried, glanced at Joanna, gave the impression that she wished she hadn't forced the issue here ; but she had, and she wasn't likely to evade an unpleasant matter.

" Tell me, Prissy," she ordered.

" I—I was with him," the maid said abruptly. Her colour had the brightness of a cock's comb in the sun. Her eyes looked like porcelain on which a bright light was shining. " I—I was out for a walk, we met in the woods and—and were just resting, and—and someone shot at him." She gulped, and began to wring her hands. " He was ever so upset, started to run after the someone, but he lost him." She stopped again, but was unable to stay silent. " I know it was a bullet ! It was buried in the tree just above our heads ; why, some of the bark fell down right on my face, I——"

She stopped, this time for good.

She had drawn the picture clearly ; vividly. She had been lying on the grass beneath a tree with George Merrow, and probably no one would ever know the whole truth of that ; how often or how they met. If her story was true, and almost certainly it was, someone had shot at them and the bullet had loosened bark which had fallen down on their faces. Merrow had jumped up and gone rushing after the sharpshooter, but had lost him.

Joanna felt strangely distressed, and heavy-hearted. It wasn't as if she didn't *know* what to expect from George Merrow.

Mrs. Baddelow's voice was unexpectedly mild.

" What happened after that, Prissy ? It's all right, I won't tell your father, not if I don't have to." Clearly she was worried ; she had seen that picture as vividly as Joanna. " Just tell me the truth."

" Well, nothing much *happened*," the maid said slowly. " He came back and said it was a pity but he thought we'd better—er—go back to the village. He escorted me to the end of the woods, then I went on alone, and he came back to the house. At least, that's what he said he was going to do. And that—that's *every*thing." But Priscilla turned a bright red again, looking at Joanna as much as Mrs. Baddelow, and cried defiantly : " There's nothing wrong in having a cuddle, is there ? "

" If there was anything wrong about it this time, I wouldn't blame you," Mrs. Baddelow said, " and I'm sure Miss Woburn wouldn't, either."

Joanna made herself say : " Of course not."

" If your father knew this he'd take the strap to you, and if Mr. Garfield knew he'd dismiss you at once, and that would end up the same way," said the housekeeper. " So you just keep this to yourself, and don't go gossiping. Understand, Prissy ? "

" I—I wouldn't *dream* of telling anyone ! "

" Mind you don't," Mrs. Baddelow commanded. " All right, you go along and turn down my bed, never mind Mr. Merrow's room tonight." She waited until the girl was outside, then called : " And shut the door behind you ! "

Priscilla closed the door so quietly that they heard hardly a sound.

Mrs. Baddelow said : " Well, what do you think of that ? " She sounded flat and worried as she dropped down on the side of Joanna's bed. Her grey hair, pulled tightly back from her forehead, made her face look more angular than it was. " I was afraid there'd be trouble when that girl got the job, I can tell a roving eye when I see one. Mr. George was born a hundred years too late ; squire's sons don't behave like that *these* days." There was no conviction in her voice. " I was against bringing her, but when Mr. Garfield's made up his mind you can't do a thing about it. Mark Wilkins spoke for her, and I suppose you know that head gardeners are as temperamental as cooks."

Joanna said: "I suppose so. Still, we don't want to make a tragedy of it, do we?"

"It's easy for you, it's not your responsibility," Mrs. Baddelow said. "If that girl gets up to anything she shouldn't I'd be the one they'd blame, it's my job to keep them out of trouble. It's not as if I didn't guess what *he* was like, is it? Mind you, it's half Prissy's fault, the way she behaves when she's out is no one's business. I only wish——"

There was a tap at the door.

Glad of the interruption, Joanna called: "Come in."

Gedde opened the door, stood on the threshold, and said quietly:

"It's Superintendent Aylmer, Miss Woburn. Mr. Garfield said that you would see him. May I tell him that you'll be down?"

As she moved across the small room, where she worked in a comfort which would have been envied by many a business executive, Joanna realised that she had never before come, knowingly, face-to-face with a detective. She had asked policemen for directions often enough, once been involved in a trivial accident; but the police as detectives were outside her sphere of experience. Perhaps because of the story she'd just heard, she felt almost nervous.

Did one shake hands?

This Superintendent Aylmer was big, dressed in Harris tweeds which made him bulky, and if he'd worn gaiters instead of baggy trousers, she would have pictured him in any market of any country town. A comfortable-looking elderly man, he had rather tired-looking eyes and a pleasant smile. He solved the first problem by holding out his hand.

"Good evening, Miss Woburn," he said, "Mr. Garfield's told me a lot about you."

"Oh, dear," she said lamely; and after that there was only one thing to add: "Not too much to my discredit, I hope."

" On the contrary," Aylmer said, the smile broadening ; somehow, it was easy to imagine the type of thing that Garfield would say. " Well, no need to keep you long, Miss Woburn, you'll be wanting your dinner. Very plucky thing you did, if you don't mind my saying so. Not a very nice job for——"

" It had to be done."

" Hm, yes, but you didn't have to do it," said Aylmer. " Well, the thing I'm anxious to know is whether you saw anyone else near the spot about the time you were there, Miss Woburn. You'd seen Mr. Merrow before, I suppose ? "

" Yes."

" And you went the long way round and he took the short cut."

" Yes."

" Why was that, Miss Woburn ? "

It would be easy to say that it was none of his business, yet she sensed that would be the wrong thing. She felt herself going red, and remembered Priscilla's scarlet flush ; that made it worse. The flushing didn't affect her voice or her manner.

" We'd had a disagreement, and preferred to go different ways. I didn't see anyone else nearby."

" Sure, Miss Woburn ? "

" I am positive."

" Well, that's a pity," said Aylmer, rubbing his chin ; she heard the scratching sound as his finger ran over the stubble. " I hoped you might have seen the devil who put those traps there. It's a funny thing, but we happen to know they weren't there half an hour or so earlier, one of the gardeners chanced to have walked that way. You didn't hear anyone, I suppose ? "

" No," said Joanna.

" Well, can't be helped," said Aylmer, " it might delay us a bit but it won't stop us from catching the beggar sooner or later. We know where the traps came from, that's a help."

She was startled.

"But if you know whose they are, surely you know who put them there."

"Different thing altogether," Aylmer assured her. "Belonged to Jeff Liddicombe, at the 'Grey Mare'. He's got an old stable turned into a saloon that's quite a museum in its way, and those old traps were on the wall to his knowledge at two o'clock today. Closing time. Jeff Liddicombe would no more put traps down than he'd use a whip to a horse, Miss Woburn, it's just one of those things that don't happen. Those traps were stolen and put down there for some purpose which isn't clear yet, but——"

"Surely to catch rabbits! Poachers——"

"Rabbits in traps that size?" Aylmer scoffed. "Can tell you're not a countrywoman. Meant for foxes, they were, and there haven't been many round here for thirty or fifty years. Mantraps, you might say. Has Mr. Merrow said anything to you to suggest he's worried about attacks on his life?"

That question came so swiftly upon the maid's story that it was like a blow in the face. Joanna didn't answer. She saw the interest quickening in Aylmer's eyes, but still didn't speak ; and she realised that her silence would almost certainly be misconstrued.

"What *has* he said?" demanded the detective.

"Nothing," Joanna answered, too quickly. "Nothing at all." If she started to explain, it would seem such a rigmarole ; and she wanted to keep out of any fending and probing, out of anything which would show George Merrow up as a Don Juan whose greatest triumphs were with little country maids. "I'm sorry, Superintendent. Even if there were anything on Mr. Merrow's mind, he wouldn't be likely to confide in me. We were not particularly close friends."

Aylmer looked at her very straightly.

"Miss Woburn," he said severely, "whatever your personal feelings or views, it is always wise to make a full statement to the police of any matter worrying you. Anything you say will be regarded as completely confidential."

" I'm sorry," she said flatly. " I can't help you."

Aylmer didn't actually call her a liar, but looked as if he restrained himself with an effort.

" Very well." He could be cold and aloof ; he was. " If you change your mind, kindly let me know." He turned his broad shoulder towards her, massive and almost menacing ; then he turned back sharply : " Have you had any association with a man named Mannering ? John Mannering ? "

Joanna hesitated.

" Miss Woburn," Aylmer said quite nastily, " it will greatly facilitate matters if you will answer my questions."

That made her angry ; less because of the question than the manner.

She was tired out ; the encounter with Merrow hadn't been pleasant, and the task of freeing his and the dog's feet had exhausted her. She didn't know that she was suffering from a form of delayed shock. Her head was aching, she wanted to get away somewhere quiet ; and she wanted this big, boorish man to stop asking questions.

" The only time I've heard of a Mr. John Mannering was by letter, just after I came here," she said stiffly. " He wrote to Mr. Garfield on business."

" Ah ! What business ? "

" That you must ask Mr. Garfield," said Joanna abruptly. " Now, unless there is anything else of importance, I must go."

He didn't answer at once ; just looked at her, as if willing her to tell him more. She wished desperately that he would leave ; she felt that if he continued to question her, even to stand and stare, she would scream.

" Has Mr. Garfield ever told you that *he* was worried about an attempt on his life ? " Aylmer demanded abruptly.

That took her so much by surprise that it strengthened her ; and her astonishment must have shown clearly, because Aylmer's manner changed, and obviously he had his answer before she said :

" Good heavens, no ! "

" If you should have the slightest indication that Mr. Garfield is worried, or in any kind of danger, please let me know at once," Aylmer said formally.

Before she answered, he was out of the room.

4

NIGHT

IT WAS A MISERABLE EVENING.

Joanna ate alone. Afterwards she expected Garfield to send for her, but no summons came. Usually she ate with George Merrow, and sometimes Garfield ate with them; invariably all three had coffee together. Now there was the quietness of unuttered fear. George, with that mauled leg, was likely to be in hospital for weeks. At this moment he was undoubtedly under morphia, perhaps on the operating table. The massive Aylmer, with his innuendo; Priscilla, with her pathetic little story—and the bullet.

It was dark.

The dining-room was huge, and only the lights at one end were on. If she was going to have to eat alone very often, it would be better to be in her own room; she usually had breakfast there. She stood up and went to the window. It was quite dark outside, but the curtains weren't drawn; Jimmy Garfield liked plenty of light to shine out; and as she stood by a tall arched window, looking through the distorting thickness of the glass into the darkness broken only near the house, she realised something that she hadn't before.

He was afraid of the dark.

Nothing seemed to move outside. She was staring in the direction of the copse, where so much had happened. Above all, she wished that the policeman hadn't talked about the possibility of danger to the old man.

What danger could there be?

Why had Garfield seemed so worried when she had gone in, earlier in the evening?

She went out of the dining-room. Gedde, who had waited at the table, came in at the other end of the room. It was warm in the high rooms and the lofty hall. She went to the front door, opening the small door set in the massive wooden double doors with their huge iron bolts. A breeze, coming off the downs, made it seem almost cool. She stood on the porch for several minutes, ears strained to catch sounds that just weren't there. In the distance she could see a few lights, from the village of Orme Hill, where Jeff Liddicombe had the 'Grey Mare'. That started her thinking about Priscilla, the story, the whole miserable business. It was a pity the innkeeper, Liddicombe, hadn't dealt with his daughter before——

Oh, be fair!

She went in.

It was nearly ten. Her head ached with a throbbing persistence which made reading out of the question. She wished she knew whether Garfield was going to send for her or not; he seldom went to bed later than ten, but this was an unusual night.

She went up to her room and undressed, put on her dressing-gown and lay on the bed, not between the sheets. The room was tall and spacious, like all the others; far too big. It was like living in a place that was double life size, although after the first few days she hadn't noticed it so much.

She began to doze.

She went to sleep.

She did not know what time it was when she woke; and, waking, heard first the scream and then the shot somewhere below her.

She heard both sounds vaguely at first, as if they were something in a nightmare, forcing themselves upon her consciousness. She lay stiff and frightened; quivering. For a few seconds she heard nothing more, and was actually telling herself that it had been a nightmare, when she heard another scream, faint through thick walls, but unmistakable.

She jumped off the bed, slipped, and pitched forward.

2

She saved herself by grabbing the bed panel, and her heart thumped wildly. As she stood there, she heard two more sounds which she knew were shots, although they came from a long way off.

She reached the door.

As she opened it, and light came through from the passage, she heard running footsteps, and then another scream which was in the form of words.

" *Stop him, stop him!* "

As she ran into the hall, she thought: " He's got a gun! " It was primitive thought, spurred by fear. She needed a weapon of some kind, and there was none she could use, except on the walls.

A dagger.

She could have her choice, but shrank from taking one and ran instead towards the running footsteps. The passage was never-ending, but now the sound of screaming had died away, there was only the running man.

She reached the hall.

The small door within the door was open wide. A man was moving towards it, staring along the passage down there, not looking up. She could see the top of his head, the small white patch, not larger than a half-crown, in the dark hair. He put a pale white hand on the door, and opened it wider. He didn't look up, and the view she had of his face was distorted. He climbed through the doorway, withdrawing his right hand last ; and in it was the gun.

For the rest, there was silence.

The door didn't close.

Joanna kept running, had paused only for the second when he had first appeared. Now she was called two ways ; to follow him, and to go and see what had happened. Fear was like a scream inside her. She reached the foot of the stairs, and felt the wind coming in from the downs.

Then she saw Gedde.

He was moving unsteadily. Blood glistened at the corner of his mouth, his eyes looked huge and glittering.

He was wearing a dark blue dressing-gown, very like his
usual black, and his face was a dirty white colour. He
held a gun in his right hand, pointing towards the door.
He tried to run, but almost fell.

"Gedde !" Joanna cried.

He looked up at her, and his mouth opened, but she
couldn't hear the words. He made a fluttering movement
with his empty hand, and she gathered that he was telling
her to go to the door and follow the man. She hesitated,
out of her dread ; and as she did so, Gedde pitched
forward, the gun struck the floor and slithered towards
her.

Gedde hit the floor so heavily that the thud of his
falling made Joanna flinch.

The gun was only a few feet away.

She rushed forward, and snatched at it, then turned
round. Gedde lay quite still, but she could picture his
movement in her mind's eye, could understand what he
wanted so desperately. She reached the door.

A red light showed, not far away.

An engine whined, with the touch of the self-starter ;
whined again and yet again, and then turned smoothly.
There was a pale white light at the front of the car, too ;
it faced the long drive and the distant gates ; the glow
of the rear light touched bushes growing close to the
drive itself.

The car began to move.

She raised the gun, and fired. She knew how to use
an automatic, but this was a revolver and it kicked so
badly that she almost dropped it. Pain throbbed at her
elbow and her shoulder. She tried to level the gun again,
and gritted her teeth as she squeezed the trigger. The
kick back didn't seem so bad ; and after the roar of the
shot, she heard a metallic clang, as if the bullet had struck
the body of the car. It did nothing to slow the car
down ; instead, it moved faster, and suddenly the headlights flashed on, illuminating the drive and stretches on
either side, the bushes, the slim trunks of young trees,
the great girth of some oaks. The pool of light was

constantly moving, the red glow fading, and the dark shape of the car was vivid against the glow.

At a turn in the drive she saw it broadside on ; then trees hid it, except for the glow which grew further and further away.

The sound of the engine died, too.

She was alone again, here ; alone with the wounded Gedde, and perhaps with death.

The wind was chilly now.

She turned, as quickly as she could make herself, fighting the fear which was never far away. Now it was not fear of what might happen to her, only of what she might find. Why hadn't the others heard ? Couldn't they, in their rooms ? Where was Mrs. Baddelow, where was Priscilla, where were the other members of the staff ? There were seven in all ; surely Gedde had managed to send for help.

Lights blazed out. Had Gedde put them on ; or the intruder ?

Silence greeted her.

Gedde was stretched out with his right hand crushed beneath him and his left flung forward, as if he were trying to stop the gun from falling. He hadn't moved. A little patch of blood, near his side, glistened in the bright light. Joanna gritted her teeth as she went towards him, hesitatingly.

She felt his pulse ; there was no hint of beating, no doubt that he was dead.

She straightened up and moved swiftly, head raised and chin thrust forward, towards Jimmy Garfield's room.

She reached it.

The door was wide open, and all the lights on ; it seemed to her that for the rest of her life she would associate death with blazing lights. The room seemed empty ; the wheel-chair was not in sight. There was no sound to ease her fears, and she made herself go further into the room. There it was, with the great glazed bookcases filled with books, the thick carpet, the

evidence of wealth in a kind of restrained opulence.
The primitive bronzes stared blindly upon it all.

The door leading to Jimmy's bedroom was open.

Had he been—in bed ?

A clock struck, startling her, and for the first time she
wondered what time it was. The striking was deep,
sonorous. One—two——

She waited.

One, two. It was two o'clock in the morning, the cold,
witching hours. The note was vibrant and its quivering
lasted for a long time, as if it wanted to be heard.

She went into the old man's room.

Yes, he was in bed.

He had been struck savagely on the head, there was
red on the pillow case, on the sheet, on his face. But he
wasn't dead. His eyes were open. He lay there helpless and, as George had been, in pain, but when he saw
her his lips moved, as if he were calling.

The sight of him, hurt but alive, put new spirit into
her, took away the dread, strengthened her and told her
what she had to do. Telephone the police and a doctor,
then go for Mrs. Baddelow.

No ! She might be able to save Jimmy's life, before
doing any of these. She reached him. His mouth was
still moving, and his blue eyes were trying to convey a
message ; she heard a sound, just a husky whisper
which did not make sense, coming from the back of his
throat.

" Don't talk, Jimmy," she said, " don't talk, I'll help
you." She was examining the wound at the side of his
head; she couldn't tell how bad it was, realised only
that there might be severe internal hæmorrhage, as well
as the bleeding she could see. Where was the right spot
to exert pressure ?

First, she needed a pad of some kind, to stem the
bleeding.

A sheet ; a pillow case ; anything.

Garfield was mouthing and making that whispering
sound.

" Jimmy," she said, quite steadily now, " don't talk, or you'll make it worse."

He ignored her.

She slid a pillow out of a slip, folded the slip, and pressed it gently on the wound, where the blood was slowly pulsing out. He was moving his right hand, towards the corner, much as Gedde had done.

" *Jimmy, lie still !* "

Suddenly, alarmingly, his voice became strong. That was so unexpected that she stopped what she was doing.

" Take the miniatures and take them to Mannering," he said. " They're in the seat of my chair. Tell no one, y'understand ? No one. Take them to John Man——"

He stopped, and his voice faded as suddenly as it had strengthened. He grabbed her hand. She sensed his fear, and shared it. His eyes were very bright and rounded, he looked at her as if pleadingly.

" Jimmy ! " she breathed.

Then his eyes closed, as if putting out a light, and his frail body sagged. After a second the tightness of his grip on her arm slackened.

" Jimmy," she breathed again.

There were tears in her eyes.

5

THE MINIATURES

JOANNA TURNED AWAY FROM THE BED AND THE STILL, lifeless figure. Lifeless? He looked dead, and for a moment she told herself that he was. She moved only a foot or two, to the telephone at the bedside table. She picked up the receiver, and, while waiting, watched Jimmy Garfield.

Was he breathing?

The village operator, a woman, said: "Number, please."

"I want—I want the police station."

"The police sta——" The woman stopped. "Do you mean the village constable, miss?"

"No, the police station in Orme, where Superintendent Aylmer is."

"Oh, *Orme*. Just hold on a minute, miss." There was a pause, then came the noises which seemed inseparable from the telephone. Then: "Oh, miss, I hope nothing's the matter. I've heard all about that awful business with the traps, poor Mr. Merrow must . . ."

Was Garfield *breathing*?

Joanna's eyes began to glisten; she thought he was. She broke across the woman's flow of words, without a thought.

"Yes, it is serious. Ask the police to come here as soon as possible, will you, with a doctor and—and an ambulance."

"*Another* ambulance? Why, what on earth——"

"Quickly, please."

Joanna put the receiver down. She felt choked, but was quite sure that she hadn't made a mistake. Jimmy was breathing, his chest was rising and falling slightly and there was a faint movement at his lips.

Jimmy, Jimmy, Jimmy !

She became almost frenzied. Get blankets, hot-water
bottles, anything to keep him warm, keep the circulation
going, she could let him die or she could save him. She
heaped blankets over him, then ran into the passage,
heading for the kitchen—and she saw Priscilla.

Priscilla was getting up from behind a big, carved
chair ; its oak had been blackened by the centuries.
She had no colour at all. She was wearing an open
dressing-gown over a pair of flimsy pyjamas, which didn't
conceal much ; and it wasn't her fault that when allowed
full freedom, her curves were riotous. She was shivering.

" Priscilla, what——"

" I—I—I heard——" Priscilla began, shrilly and then
broke off. " I heard a—a bang, and came down,
and——"

Her mouth worked, like an idiot's.

" Priscilla ! Go and put a kettle on, at once ! Fill
two hot-water bottles. Bring them here. Then call
Mrs. Baddelow. Understand ? "

" I—I—I heard——"

" *Go for those hot-water bottles !* "

Priscilla turned away. She did not need to pass
Gedde, although the sight of him had affected her so
badly. She faltered, but gradually gained courage ; or
appeared to. At last she disappeared. Joanna turned
back into the room, flinched at the sight of the still
figure, and wondered if she had been dreaming.

She glanced at the wheel-chair.

She felt as if Jimmy Garfield had charged her with a
mission, with his dying breath. She was to take the
miniatures hidden in his wheel-chair to John Mannering
—the man in whom Aylmer was so interested.

She couldn't think about that now.

Jimmy hadn't stirred, and it was easy to believe that
she had been wrong, that blankets and hot-water bottles
would do no good at all.

She could only wait.

She went to the wheel-chair, and saw nothing unusual ;

but she knew that the padded seat was removable ; it was fastened with straps. She unfastened the straps and lifted it. There was a flat box which fitted flush with the sides of the chair, almost as if it had been made for it. She lifted this out, and saw that it was heavily sealed with Sellotape. She didn't try to open it, but put it on one side, replaced the chair seat, and pushed the chair further away. She hesitated, then turned and went out, hurrying up to her room. She put the box beneath the mattress at the foot of her bed, then went downstairs again. She reached the door of Jimmy Garfield's room as a man came hurrying from the service quarters—an odd-job man in his sixties, looking scared.

" You all right, Miss Woburn ? " He was breathless. " That Prissy's in such a state I don't know whether to believe her or not. I haven't called the others—shall I, or——"

He caught sight of Gedde, and his voice trailed off.

Two minutes later, Priscilla arrived with tears streaming down her face from the reaction—but with the hot-water bottles under her arm.

The puzzling thing was that Mrs. Baddelow still wasn't here, but there was no time to worry about Mrs. Baddelow or anyone. Joanna put the hot-water bottles in with Jimmy, one on each side of the frail body, and then turned her attention to Priscilla, who was heading for an attack of hysterics which wouldn't help at all. She needed a hot drink, some clothes on, much reassurance.

There was too much to do.

At least it saved Joanna from thinking.

She was surprised that the police arrived so quickly. First, two men in uniform, with a car bearing the illu-minated sign *Police* on the roof ; then the ambulance with another policeman by the side of the driver ; finally, Aylmer and two other plain-clothes men and a police-surgeon, a white-haired daddy of a man who sounded asthmatic. It was Aylmer who took complete control, talked to Joanna briefly and mildly, nodded as if he fully understood, and somehow reassured her. By then she was feeling dreadful; shivering fits kept coming over her, and she couldn't stop them. The doctor made her up a milky looking white dose, and ten minutes after she'd taken it, she felt steadier.

Yet she did not see what happened moment by moment. So much was going on. The police-surgeon with Jimmy, with Gedde, with Priscilla; the police, searching everywhere; police-cars with their headlights blazing, at the spot on the drive where the little car had stood while she had shot at it. The police with the gun Joanna herself had fired; talking to her again, and drawing her story out quietly, item by item.

Then, highlights:

" No, Mr. Garfield's not dead," the white-haired daddy said, " but he is gravely injured, no point in minimising the danger. We'll do all we can."

At least, there were some grounds for hope.

" I don't think you need worry about Mrs. Baddelow," said Aylmer, " apparently she is used to taking a sleeping draught, there are tablets by her bed. Dr. Menzies thinks that she took more than usual last night, and she is simply in a drugged sleep. No great harm's done."

Then, a few minutes later: " Glad to tell you that Mr. Merrow is comfortable, anyhow."

" Oh, good ! " That delighted her; and in a queer way told her that she had missed him dreadfully in the night's nightmare.

Finally : " Now I'm going to recommend that *you* have a sleeping draught, Miss Woburn, and go to bed. You'll feel twice the woman you are if you can sleep the clock round. We shall be here all night and well into the morning, so you'll have nothing to worry about."

" Thank you," Joanna said, almost stupidly. " Thank you. If I can just lie down that will be fine. I'm sure I shall sleep."

" Of course you will," Aylmer reassured her. " But the draught will make sure you don't wake up too soon ! " He actually took her along to her room; and she realised that he had shielded her from Priscilla and the other servants, had made sure that she wasn't harassed more than the circumstances compelled. " No way in which you can help us further, is there ? Nothing indicated what the thief came after ? " he asked in his deep, almost ponderous voice.

" Absolutely nothing," Joanna said.

She remembered the first meeting with Aylmer, and his grimness, as she went to her bed and dropped heavily on to it. She pressed her hands against her forehead, looked at him, but said almost to herself : " I should have told this afternoon . . ."

She told him now ; all Priscilla's story.

Aylmer listened intently and without interrupting. When she had finished, he said :

" Ah, hum, yes. Understand your reticence." Not a word of rebuke, not even a hint of it. " Well, if we can't get at the truth any other way we'll have to question young Prissy Liddicombe." He grinned. " Pert little piece, that lass, if her father used the strap on her a bit more and talked less about what he was going to do, she'd be more like. All right, Miss Woburn, thanks for telling me. Good-night."

He went out.

When she got into bed she thought that she would never sleep.

When she woke it was after midday.

Her mind was quite clear, and she remembered every-thing, although not too vividly. The daddy-doctor had known what he was about, obviously, for the draught had not only made her sleep, but had soothed her nerves. She could recollect what had happened without any feeling of horror.

When she went out, wearing just her dressing-gown, a policeman was on duty at the end of the passage, and gave her a stolid ' good-morning '. When she returned, Mrs. Baddelow was in her room, looking as severe as ever until the door closed, and then becoming almost tearful.

"Oh, 1 wouldn't have let you bear the burden of this on your own for *any*thing; if I'd dreamt of what might happen I wouldn't have cared if I hadn't slept a wink. I sleep so badly, dear, you don't know what that is until you've suffered from insomnia for a year or two, and Gedde had been so difficult for the past few days. Then there was Prissy. I felt *des*perate, so I took two tablets. But I've *never* slept so heavily as that before, and——"

"It doesn't matter." Joanna stopped the flood. "Don't worry about it. If there could be a cup of tea . . ."

"Oh, of *course*!" Mrs. Baddelow hurried out.

Joanna felt beneath the mattress for the flat box. It was still there. She turned it over in her hand, and wondered exactly how much it was worth, and why Jimmy had charged her with taking it to Mannering. She asked herself if she ought to tell the police, but at heart knew that she wouldn't; there had been the old man's talk of a twenty-year burden on his conscience; and his tone when he had said there were not many whom he could trust.

She *must* be trustworthy.

Mrs. Baddelow brought the tea herself.

"And I've just rung the hospital, dear; the report isn't *too* bad. At least he's just hanging on, poor old chap." She stood quite still, hands clasped in front of her flat waist. "I do hope he doesn't die, this is the best job I've had for years. Well, you take it easy, dear, no one's going to complain if you stay in bed all day."

Joanna didn't want to stay in bed all day. She wanted to take that box to John Mannering. It would mean going to London, and giving some reason why she wanted to, and she turned it over in her mind during the afternoon. Aylmer wasn't at the house, but the other police were still searching for clues; there was no news of an arrest, no further news of Jimmy.

She went through the files, and found the letter which

Mannering had sent, from Quinns, Hart Row, London, W.1. It simply asked if he were interested in two Ming vases, and gave the dimensions; Jimmy had politely said ' no '. The notepaper was of excellent quality and the address, together with the words *Antiques—Objets d'Art*, were embossed in black. She filed the letter again, and then began to worry about how to go to London. She had no car, but Jimmy had allowed her to use a little Austin runabout, although she'd always asked permission.

She couldn't, now.

She could tell Aylmer that she had business in London; letters in the files showed that she was here on a month's trial, and that the month was up today. Thirty days of quiet hopefulness, the enjoyment marred only by George Merrow, and one day of violence touched with horror. Now——

She stopped herself thinking about it.

She went to ask the policeman in charge if there were any objection to her keeping an appointment in London, and found him in the library, talking to a man she hadn't seen before. The stranger was tall, almost startlingly good-looking, with a smile which attracted and a voice which pleased. When she entered, this man glanced at her. She liked him on sight, and sensed that he would move well, that he carried much authority.

Could he be from Scotland Yard?

The local man turned, and said : " Hallo, Miss Woburn, how can I help you ? " Before she had a chance to answer, he went on : " Do you know Mr. Mannering ? "

She knew that her surprise showed in her expression, knew that it puzzled both men, and her ' no ' had a strangely false ring.

6

A MAN TO TRUST?

MANNERING WAS OBVIOUSLY A MAN TO LIKE; AND looked a man to trust. His manner and his movements reminded Joanna of George Merrow, but he had something that Merrow lacked; complete assurance. George had a chip on his shoulder; this man hadn't.

He put her at her ease in a word or two.

"I've been asking Inspector Hill if I could worry you for a few minutes' talk, Miss Woburn. When is a good time for you?"

"Whenever you like."

"That's fine," Mannering said. "Do you think——"

"Let me get a question in first," interrupted the detective named Hill. "Did you know that Mr. Garfield was in touch with Mr. Mannering by telephone last night, Miss Woburn?"

"I'd no idea." Joanna was astonished.

"Did you expect him to send for Mr. Mannering?"

"No."

Hill seemed to shrug. "It's a puzzle, Mr. Mannering—but unless Mr. Garfield comes round, I'm afraid we shan't know what he wanted you for."

Mannering explained: "He asked me to come and see him this afternoon, Miss Woburn, and presumably it was on business. Perhaps he was thinking of buying or selling through me at Quinns."

"I just don't know," Joanna said. She wished that Hill would go; two minutes would be enough for her to tell Mannering about the box, but getting it to him might not be too easy. She began to wonder whether it would be wise to talk to him now; the police seemed to be everywhere.

"Nothing more we can do to help, Mr. Mannering,"

Hill said. It might have been Joanna's imagination, but he seemed antagonistic to Mannering; as Aylmer had been to the name. "If anything that affects you does transpire, I'll let you know."

Mannering grinned attractively.

"Thanks."

"If you'll come into my room," Joanna said, "I'll send for some tea."

She led the way. Three of the plainclothes men looked intently at Mannering, and one was obviously pointing him out to the others. The impression that they were antagonistic, perhaps wary, remained; in spite of her liking for the man, her doubts of him rose. Yet Jimmy had been emphatic.

She offered him a chair and cigarettes, and rang the bell for a maid; Priscilla came. The girl looked pale and her make-up was conspicuous by its absence, but at sight of Mannering her eyes lit up; the handsome male would always raise her spirits. She glanced round from the door.

Joanna felt that she positively disliked the girl.

"How can I help you, Mr. Mannering?"

"I'm not a bit sure that you can," Mannering said, "but I'd like to find out what Jimmy wanted me for." She was surprised at the 'Jimmy'. "You've really no idea at all?"

She hesitated.

He watched her, smiling, giving her the impression that he guessed the cause of her uncertainty. He didn't try to hurry her, but sat in a winged armchair as if he were thoroughly at home.

She said at last: "Yes, I have an idea. I'm worried about it, but he—he was quite definite." It was very easy now that the ice was broken. "He came round before the police reached here last night, and asked me to give you a box—he said that it contained miniatures." She was sitting at her desk, one hand resting lightly on the table, honey-brown eyes almost the same colour as Mannering's. "I have the box in my bedroom."

" And you haven't told the police about it ? "

" No."

" Why not ? "

" Jimmy said I was to tell no one."

Mannering looked at her hard, and then said softly :
" Lucky Jimmy. Have you opened the box ? "

" No."

Mannering said : " It would be a mistake to let me
have-it here. You may not believe it, but the police
get peculiar ideas about my integrity, and *might* search
my car." He smiled broadly. " One of the drawbacks
of being an interfering amateur ! Is there any chance
of you coming to London in the next day or two ? "

" I want to come this evening, and stay in town over-
night, if the police have no objection."

" They won't have," Mannering assured her. " No
reason why they should." His smile encouraged her.
" Have you any sound reason for visiting London ? "

" I thought of pretending to have an appointment
with a prospective employer," she said. " My month's
trial was up today, it—it sounds reasonable."

Mannering nodded.

" I don't want to tell them about Jimmy and the box,"
Joanna went on. " Do *you* know more than you told
the police ? "

She could understand Hill's silent antagonism, now.

" Possibly just a little more," admitted Mannering,
and something in his manner made her want to laugh.
" The police certainly regard me with the darkest suspicion, you've undoubtedly noticed that. Jimmy Garfield
knew, that's probably why he contacted me." That came
out dryly. " What time are you free to leave here ? "

" It's up to the police."

" Let's suggest five o'clock," Mannering said. " I can
leave at half-past four, and be in London well ahead of
you. Perhaps you'd better bring the box to my flat,
instead of Quinns, the police might follow you—or even
be keeping an eye on Quinns ! " His smile flashed again.
" Reprobate, aren't I ? "

" Obviously ! "

For an odd reason, he cheered her up.

Priscilla came in, with the tea. A plainclothes man was just outside the door, and Joanna had an uncomfortable feeling that he'd been listening. There was no way of finding out.

Mannering left a little before half-past four.

Hill showed no surprise and asked no questions when Joanna spoke about going to London. She was free to go wherever she wished. Walking down the huge staircase with a small suitcase containing the box and a few personal oddments, she felt acutely self-conscious, but none of the police appeared to be interested in her. There were very few in the house now ; as nearly as it could be, the situation was back to normal.

Jimmy, she knew, was still unconscious.

George Merrow was ' comfortable '.

She took the wheel of the grey runabout, and drove towards the end of the drive, feeling the rush of cool wind round her head, for the drop-head roof was down. Two gardeners were working as if nothing had happened, and old Wilkins waved to her. Her mind soon turned to the steel traps taken from the ' museum ' at the ' Grey Mare ', to Priscilla and her father, and by degrees to the awful business last night.

Driving helped her.

The engine purred smoothly, the road surface was good, the sun was pleasantly warm, the countryside could hardly have looked better. It was an hour and a half's drive to London, and Mannering had told her not to worry whatever time she arrived at his flat in Green Street, Chelsea ; she should be there about half-past six.

There was little traffic on this by-road. Orme village was six miles behind her, the next town eleven miles ahead, and only two small villages lay between.

Trees grew straight and slender on either side of the road, two miles from the gates of Brook House. It was one of the straightest and most pleasant parts of the drive, soothing enough to lull her into a sense of quiet and reassurance. Mannering had helped a great deal, talking to him had relieved her mind, and once he had the box there would be nothing to worry about ; well, nothing for her to worry about.

She turned a corner, and her heart leapt wildly.

A big car was drawn up across the road, only twenty yards ahead. It was slewed across, and there wasn't a hope of squeezing past. A man stood on the far side of the car, another by the trees.

As she caught sight of them all, Joanna felt a new horror ; they were watching, they had planned to make her crash.

She jammed on the brakes. The car jolted, tyres screamed, the engine stalled—but the car slithered forward, now straight ahead, now broadside on, travelling with sickening speed and carrying her to the inevitable crash. She didn't see the men, now, just the side of the big car, the sun shimmering on the window, the massive black side looking like a great steel wall.

The Austin slithered, and spun round. The back of the car caught the black car on one wing ; there was a frightening crash, and Joanna was thrown forward, the steering wheel struck her painfully and her head banged on the windscreen.

She didn't lose consciousness.

Her head was whirling when she tried to look about her. Figures moved ; of men, running towards her. One of them looked very pale, but she was only half aware of that. She felt at screaming pitch, felt quite certain that they wanted the square box.

She turned, thrust an arm over the back of the seat, and snatched up the case. Then she realised she was drawing attention to it, but she couldn't leave it behind. The men were still a yard or two away. She flung open the door and jumped out. Here, the men were facing her, she hadn't a chance to escape. She stood there, gripping the suitcase and glaring at them, longing desperately for another car to come ; but there was only silence.

The larger of the two men said : " Take it easy, and hand over that bag." His voice had a metallic timbre and he looked strange ; bony.

She didn't speak.

" If you don't want to get hurt," the man said, " you will do what I say. Don't expect any help. I have put a man with a red flag holding up the traffic round the corner *and* the other side of the car. No one will see you." He drew a step nearer. He looked big and powerful and uncanny, with a kind of made-up face. His right hand was stretched out, to take the bag ; he felt quite sure that she would surrender it.

She raised it, and made a wild swing at him. He dodged, but a corner caught his shoulder, and sent him staggering. The smaller man jumped forward, but couldn't get out of the staggering man's way. Joanna darted past, towards the corner, towards the man with the red flag and any motorist who might be coming. Fear turned to terror. The unreal nightmare world had no end, she felt trapped—as George had been in the copse, as—Jimmy.

She heard movement behind her.

She was almost at the corner when the smaller of the two men reached her, grabbing her left arm. The case was heavy in her right hand, and she couldn't fling it ; she couldn't get away. She was sobbing with pain and with frustration, and her terror was a living thing, vivid as the fear of death. The man had a grip on her wrist which she couldn't break, and was forcing her to slow down.

Then, he tripped her.

She went sprawling. The case saved her from the worst of the fall, but it knocked the breath out of her. The case fell and slithered along the tarred road, as Gedde's gun had slithered along the stone passage the night before. *Gedde had been dying.* She tried to pick herself up, but couldn't ; she felt pain all over. She gritted her teeth and dragged herself to her knees—as the big man snatched the case, and the smaller man said :

" . . . little vixen. What are we going to do ? "

" Only one thing to do," the large man said. She couldn't see him now, could only hear his grating voice. " Put her back near the car and smash her up. Now she's seen us we can't let her go."

He stopped.

Not far off, there was a new sound ; the sound of a car engine, of someone approaching.

Then, as if they were uttered again, she heard the thing that the big man had said : " *Put her back near the car and smash her up. Now she's seen us we can't let her go.*"

They were going to kill her.

She felt her arm gripped from behind, then thrust upwards. She couldn't move except under the brute's pressure. He dragged her to her feet. The sound of the other car grew louder, the pressure of the man's hand grew tighter, and she was thrust towards the runabout.

" *Put her back near the car and smash her up.*"

She screamed.

7

JOHN MANNERING SAYS . . .

AS SOON AS THE SCREAM FORCED ITS WAY OUT, JOANNA felt herself thrust to one side. Then a hand was clapped over her mouth, stifling the sound. She was lifted bodily and carried towards the cars. Terrified as she was, she sensed desperation in the way the men were behaving; fear was driving them as well as her.

She was only half conscious, but knew exactly what they were planning to do—and she couldn't lift a finger to help herself.

Then she saw the big car moving.

A man sat at the wheel, reversing; the smash hadn't damaged it much.

" Knock her out, push her under," the large man's voice seemed to clang. " It's our only chance."

She felt a blow on the side of the head, but didn't quite lose consciousness. She felt herself lowered to the ground, then stretched out on her back. It was the most hideous thing she could have conceived; there she was, on the road, and the engine of the big car was roaring as if it were straining at a leash, desperate to leap at her, to crush the life out of her.

She couldn't scream.

She tried to scramble to her feet, to get out of the way, to do anything to save herself. The wheels of the car were only a few feet away, she could see the undercarriage, dark and menacing, the roar of the engine was deafening. She couldn't move fast enough, there just wasn't a hope.

She heard a sharp, explosive sound.

She didn't know what it was. Vaguely she was aware that the car quivered, but it didn't stop moving. It seemed to change its direction, as if it were chasing her.

She couldn't do a thing, could only crouch there, expecting the impact any second.

It didn't come.

The car had stopped.

The driver was jumping out, on the other side. She heard the men near her running away, and shouting. She heard new sounds, too; as if men were shooting. She wasn't sure. All she knew for certain was that she was alive, the killer car was lurching to one side, some men were running, and someone was running towards her.

One of the—*murderers*?

She put her hands up, to fend them off, and through her shaking fingers she saw John Mannering.

Mannering flung himself forward, and Joanna sensed that he was trying to shelter her with his body. She heard a confusion of sounds, and felt the weight as he pressed against her. The light of day was shut out, her face was pressed against his coat.

In those few seconds, Mannering saw men driving off in a big Austin; and saw police, who had been some distance behind him, coming to help and to chase; but they would be too late.

He stood up, and another man knelt by Joanna's side. For a long time she hardly knew what it was all about, her head felt so bad.

Then, hazily, she remembered the black box in the suitcase.

Had it gone?

She looked about, desperately, and saw no sign of it. She'd lost it. The police began to ask questions.

She felt too dispirited and low to keep anything back, Aylmer as well as Mannering was present when she told them what she had been doing with the flat box.

John Mannering listened to Joanna Woburn's story, and glanced occasionally at Aylmer. Whatever Aylmer thought, he kept to himself.

The road had been cleared, traffic was passing, and police were making sure that no curious driver stopped to stare at the congregation of cars, or at the girl who was lying on the verge at the roadside.

One bandit car had escaped, with all four men ; the other, the large Austin, was in police hands ; it might yield clues.

Except that she hadn't any colour, and there were two or three graze marks on her temple, Joanna looked all right. She must be in the late twenties or early thirties, Mannering thought. She was fine-looking, in a clear, Scandinavian way, with her coiled hair and good skin and well-defined bone formation ; a good subject for his wife to paint. Mannering didn't think more about his wife, then, but watched Aylmer and the ' girl ', and commented only when Aylmer arranged for her to be driven back to Brook House.

" I'll see you before long," Mannering promised her. He couldn't be sure whether she heard, or whether she cared.

He watched her being driven off.

Aylmer cleared his throat. There was plenty of hostility in his eyes, but he didn't voice it ; he actually proffered cigarettes and, when they had lit up, said gruffly :

" Well, if it hadn't been for you, they'd have killed her. And you weren't to know they wouldn't shoot again, either. What makes a chap like you play detective and go all out to rub us up the wrong way, Mr. Mannering ?"

Mannering said : " It just happens, Superintendent ! I've no evil intent." He was pleasantly conversational. " Take this case. Garfield telephoned me, said that he wanted to see me on a highly confidential matter, and made an appointment for this afternoon. I came without knowing what had happened. While I'm at his house, his secretary tells me, in confidence, that Garfield told her to give me this box which is said to contain miniatures. That makes her the agent of my client, and if I have to respect his confidence, I have to respect hers.

What do you expect me to do—tell you everything, without considering the client's interests ? What would you think of me, if I did ? " He chuckled. " What do you think of the *genus* squealer ? "

As if reluctantly, Aylmer smiled back.

" I see what you mean. And you didn't know about this box and these miniatures before ? "

" I did not."

" Hmm. Well, they've gone, anyway." Aylmer ruminated. " With a bit of luck we'll catch the beggars soon, though. Recognise them ? "

" They were strangers to me."

" According to Miss Woburn, they were going to run her over so that she couldn't describe them," Aylmer said. " Then you turned up—how they missed hitting you, I don't know ! " He paused. " Well, you scared 'em off, and put a bullet through a rear tyre, so they had to crowd into one car. Sure you didn't recognise them ? " he repeated abruptly.

" Quite sure."

" Well, you'd better keep your eyes open, they looked as if they meant business ! " Aylmer's smile wasn't at all amused. " What made you turn back on the road ? "

" I first thought that if anyone was going to try to hold Miss Woburn up, it would be further down the road—you know the spot where the new road's been cut through the hill. I was on top of the cut, looking down, and saw the two cars pass. When no other traffic came along in the other direction for ten minutes, I started to get uneasy. I drove back, and saw the man with the red flag. He hadn't been there when I passed. My cue."

" I see," said Aylmer heavily. " And Miss Woburn had told you about the box, so you half-expected trouble. Who d'you think knew ? "

" I wondered who might guess that Garfield told Miss Woburn what to do if anything stopped him from doing it himself."

" I was talking to Superintendent Bristow of the Yard last night. You were mentioned, and he said there

wasn't a situation you couldn't talk yourself out of."
Aylmer sounded rueful. "All I can say is, they're
murderous devils and that girl owes her life to you.
What are you going to do now ? "

"What I'd like to do is talk to George Merrow,"
Mannering said thoughtfully. "Is he well enough yet ? "

"As a matter of fact, that leg's giving him trouble,"
Aylmer demurred. "Haven't talked to him properly myself yet. He says he doesn't know a thing." Aylmer
sniffed. "Can't tell, with you smooth types. When are
you going to see Miss Woburn again ? "

"As soon as she's better. No one's going to worry
her much now," Mannering said ; "the pair whom she
can recognise won't ask for trouble. I may come down
tomorrow afternoon some time—now I'll get back to
Town, if that's all right with you."

"Yes, I'd much rather the Yard had you to worry
about," Aylmer said dryly. "I must say they've got
your measure."

Mannering chuckled.

His car was parked on the verge fifty yards away.
Aylmer walked to it with him, as if anxious to make
sure that this time he did really leave. He was soon
driving along the narrow road, seeing the police and the
cars getting smaller and smaller in his driving mirror.
He turned a corner, and they were cut off from sight.

He drove through the defile, recently cut in brown sand-
stone rock. Beyond it, this road ran into the main
London–Horsham Road, and there was much more
traffic. He put on speed. No one took any interest in
him and he had plenty of time to think.

In fact, he knew little more than he'd told the police,
and the one thing he had kept to himself would not have
helped them. Jimmy Garfield, who had been a frequent
visitor to Quinns before the accident to his spine, had
telephoned Quinns ten days earlier, with a simple story.
He said that he was being threatened by telephone and
by letter, and that he didn't want to ask the police for
help. Would Mannering assist him ?

Mannering had been out of the country, with his wife.

Garfield had telephoned his flat last night, when Mannering had been home only for a day. The story then wasn't greatly different, except :

" I've had a load on my conscience for twenty years, Mannering, and I think it's catching up with me," Garfield had said. " Time an old man like me made retribution, eh ? Like your help. Could be dangerous. Come and see me, will you ? "

" I'm really sorry," Mannering had said, " but I'm too busy for a week or more. I will, when . . ."

" If you leave it, you'll be in time for the inquest," the old man had said cryptically.

Had he meant an inquest on himself ?

Joanna Woburn would be a long time getting over the effect of what had happened ; Garfield might never recover ; the contents of the flat box might never be found.

Face *facts*.

Since the attack on Garfield last night, Garfield's enemies had acted with a violent ruthlessness as effective as it was rare. The police weren't keyed-up to cope. Mannering saw it as a desperate, daring attempt to get some major prize. It had been skilfully planned, too. The old car, recently stolen ; the men to ward off traffic ; and another, fast car at hand, to take the men out of immediate danger.

Only he and Joanna Woburn had seen them.

He didn't take the danger from that seriously, then, although he didn't ignore it.

If Garfield recovered, he might learn much more.

If Garfield died, he might never know anything else about the case.

He could only guess——

That Garfield's enemies had meant to get the flat box at all costs, and having failed at the house, had planned the attack on Joanna——

Guessing she would have the box ?

Or knowing.

If anyone else at the house had been spying on her, word

might have been sent through to her attackers. It was even possible that someone knew that Jimmy Garfield had taken her into his confidence, or had seen her take that box.

If so, who ?

And where did he, Mannering, come in ? If he had a commission, it was to ease Garfield's conscience; and that might be much easier already.

He didn't see that there was much else he could do; certainly not now. The police were in full cry after the box and the 'miniatures'; he didn't know a thing about them, so it was useless making inquiries through the trade. Except that he had saved Joanna Woburn's life—and he told himself that was an exaggeration, for the police had arrived only a few minutes later. They had been following the girl, not dreaming of trouble on the road, only interested in finding out where she went to.

An old man, dying.

A young man, crippled and out of action for weeks.

A strikingly attractive woman with a strong sense of loyalty, presumably as much in the air as Mannering.

It wasn't the first and it wouldn't be the last unsatisfactory job. He felt sorry for Joanna Woburn, but she wasn't the type to feel sorry for herself for long. He began to whistle softly. If he had half a chance to help any of the people involved, he'd take it. Probably it would just fade out.

He did not know that two men were plotting, at that moment, to kill both him and Joanna Woburn.

Lucien Seale, a large, bony man who had a cold aloofness when meeting strangers, and who was almost a stranger to his intimates, carried the black box out of the taxi which had stopped at Horsham station, and went into the booking hall. The small man who had been with him during the attack on Joanna also got out, but they didn't travel together. These two had left the escape car, in which the two red-flag men had driven off.

Seale made quite sure that no one took any particular

interest in him, then booked a first-class single to Victoria.
He strolled on to the platform. A train was due in ten
minutes, and half a dozen people waited about. Seale
bought an early London newspaper, and stood by the
bookstall, from where he could see the ticket barrier
on this platform and on the other side. No one who
worried him arrived.

With the box under his arm, wrapped in the *Evening
News*, he caught the train. He had a first-class carriage
to himself as far as Guildford, where a young couple
and an old man got in. Beyond a first cursory glance,
none of these looked at Lucien Seale.

Inwardly, he relaxed.

At Victoria, he was very careful indeed, and it was over
a quarter of an hour before he left in a taxi which he
picked up outside the station. When he reached his
house, near Hampstead Heath, it was a little after eight
o'clock, and nearly dark. No one else was there, and
he let himself in with a key.

The house was silent.

He walked up to the first floor, with the flat box still
under his arm, and entered a room which looked more
like an office than a study; was furnished in sharp,
modern lines. It had a window overlooking a long,
narrow back garden, and the garden and house in the
next road. Net curtains were placed across the window
so that it was impossible for anyone to look in.

He did not open the box.

He had been in the house for five minutes when the
telephone bell rang.

" Hallo," he said, and listened carefully. " Yes, come
at once. Make sure you are alone."

He put the receiver down, and then went slowly to
another room at the front of the house. This was also
curtained so that it couldn't be overlooked, but he could
see out. The front garden was long and narrow, and
on the other side of the road there were the walls of a
large garden surrounding a big house, darkening in the
evening light. No one stood watching.

When the small man who had been with him at Horsham station arrived, he drove up in a small car.

He wasn't followed.

He also let himself in with a key, and the two men met at the head of the stairs.

They made a sharp contrast.

The large man's face was very thin, had a bony, almost hungry look. His high cheekbones suggested that his ancestry wasn't all British. He had a curious stealth of movement, and a fixed gaze. The impression that strangers had of him was his lack of humanity. He hardly looked real, but he was real enough, no one was ever likely to like him as a person.

The other was round-faced, chubby, rather a pleasant-looking little man, with round eyes and a soft little mouth, and a bald spot in dark hair. He would have been at home in any bar or night club, or on any dance-floor. There was nothing robot-like about him, yet when he met the large man, there was similarity ; one of tension.

" Heard from the others ? " the chubby man asked.

" No."

" They'll be all right."

" I am not at all sure that they'll be all right," said Lucien Seale. " I see no point in refusing to see the possibility of danger. If it had been handled properly, all would be well. I had arranged for Merrow to be attacked, and that the old man would do everything he could to save Merrow. And he would have. But when Pete lost his head, and killed Gedde and nearly killed the old man, we were in trouble. We wanted the old man alive, and——"

" You know how it was," Greer said slowly. " Gedde came along, Pete lost his head and hit the old man too hard. But you worry too much, Lucien."

" I always worry enough," Lucien Seale told him, and his lips moved with great precision ; greatly exaggerated, it would have looked like a ventriloquist's doll talking. " And whether they are safe or not, we still have a grave problem. Mannering and the girl saw me."

' Me '.

The man named Greer didn't speak.

" I dare not risk being recognised," Seale said. " There is enough in that box to put me inside for the rest of my life. You know that. Mannering probably knows, as the old man sent for his help. The woman Joanna might know. I can't take risks on being recognised. We have to decide how best and how quickly we can kill them." That came out quite flatly. " Mannering must be dealt with first ; he could be as dangerous as the police. He would search for me, I wouldn't dare show my face. The girl—she can wait for a little while." Seale placed one large, knuckly hand on the top of the newel post at the head of the stairs, and went on coldly : " We should deal with Mannering tonight."

" But he'll be on the look-out," Greer began. " He may not have *seen* the photostats, may not know——"

" Tonight," Seale said coldly. " It's too big a risk, we can't wait."

8

THE MANNERINGS

LORNA MANNERING HEARD THE CAR TURN INTO THE street, looked out, recognised John's Rolls-Bentley and stood at the window, looking down and feeling almost as eager as she had done when they had first come to live here; after their honeymoon. She craned her neck, so that she could see him get out, watched the way he closed the door and turned, glancing up as if hoping to catch a glimpse of her.

He felt just about as she did.

She was wearing a black cocktail dress, trimmed with red. She looked lovely, and knew it. If a few strands of grey touched her wavy dark hair, it didn't matter; if there was a hint of wrinkles at her eyes, that didn't matter. There was the quality of youthfulness about her. She moved to the door, and opened it as he came up the last flight of stairs. This studio flat was at the top of a narrow, four-storied house in Green Street, and it overlooked the distant Thames, for houses rased by the bombing hadn't been rebuilt.

Mannering paused, eyes widening. "My, my! Who's been taking years off your age?"

Lorna laughed; if he'd tried for a week he couldn't have touched a better phrase.

"Approved?"

"Dior himself would approve."

"It's a new dressmaker at a quarter of the price," Lorna said; "I hope she isn't discovered too soon, it'll go to her head." She kissed him. "We're going out to dinner."

His face dropped.

" Oh, Lor'. Not social ? "

" Alone," said Lorna. " Ethel twisted her ankle this
afternoon. It's nothing serious, but she ought to rest
up for a few days. So we'll snack whenever we're at
home, and have the main meals out."

" Oh, well," said Mannering resignedly. " I suppose
we can't have everything in one seductive body, painter,
wife and cook." He went into his study and opened a
cocktail cabinet which was in fact an old Jacobean court
cupboard. " Need I change ? "

" No. You look a bit down, darling."

" Things went wrong, and I can't see any way of
putting 'em right." Mannering poured whisky for himself, sherry for Lorna, and as they drank, told her what
had happened and what conclusion he had reached.
She knew that the case would nag at him until it died
a natural death or until he saw some way of helping the
injured man or Joanna Woburn.

" As far as I can tell they've got what they wanted,
and they'll lie low for a bit and then come up for air
again," Mannering said. " If the police pick 'em up I'll
be able to identify them, but——" He shrugged.

" 'Nother ? "

" No, thanks. You have a quick one, and I'll
drive ! "

He grinned. " We'll go by taxi."

In fact, they went by taxi, so that there would be no
parking problem. The ' Lion and the Lamb ', in Grex
Street, Soho, was small, reputable, amiable and had
excellent food and a really good band. But Mannering
wasn't dancing as he could and should be. By half-past
eleven, Lorna said :

" Let's get home, darling."——

" Mind ? "

" I could do with an early night, too."

" Fine," Mannering said, and paid the bill and left,
with the proprietor begging him to return and half a
dozen youngsters pointing him out as *the* John Mannering,
" the antique-dealer detective, you know ". They

stepped into the warm, starlit evening, and Mannering hailed a taxi. They got in.

A man on a motor-cycle followed them.

The one cure for the doldrums, Mannering knew well, was Lorna. The dancing hadn't helped; sitting back in the cab, with Lorna's hand in his, helped a lot. The simple delights. They were near Chelsea Town Hall when he tapped at the glass partition, and told the driver to take them to the Embankment. It was a good night for a walk; cool, pleasant. He noticed the motor-cycle roar past them, and had been vaguely aware of one pop-popping in his ear for some time. Motor-cycles were two a penny and he didn't give this one a second thought.

A motor-cycle was parked against the wall of a house when they reached the Embankment. He noticed this, without giving it a thought, either. The massive block of the Battersea Power Station, just across the river, was showing clearly in floodlighting. Dense white smoke rolled from one of its huge chimneys. The floodlighting reflected on the Thames. So did the fairy lights at the Pleasure Garden, sole surviving relic this far up river of the great Festival. Lights of all colours were still on their stands, but seemed to dance in the water.

Lights from the bridges in sight were reflected too. A launch, probably with police in it, was moving slowly up-river. Odd traffic passed up and down the Embankment, including several motor-cycles; and he gave none of these a thought.

They strolled towards Green Street, watching the river.

They did not see the man who walked on the pavement across the road, sometimes ahead of them, and sometimes a few yards behind them.

"It's a perfect night," Lorna said quietly. "Just right." She spoke for the sake of speaking, for words didn't really matter. Mannering's arm was round her

3

waist, his hand resting lightly. They walked in step, very conscious of one another's nearness. Mannering murmured something which didn't count. The stars looked down on them, the traffic passed, and death drew nearer.

Green Street was only a hundred yards away. Had there been a light in his study, the kitchen or the studio, they would have been able to see it ; but they could not yet see even the outline of the top of the house. They kept near the parapet, where it was reinforced after the floods of a year or two before, reluctant to cross over. The mood would probably break as soon as they got indoors, and Lorna longed for some way of preserving it.

Reluctantly she said :

" Case still on your mind ? "

" It is, rather."

" You might see daylight tomorrow."

He smiled unexpectedly : " Ever the optimist ! I don't think so, I'm afraid——"

He didn't finish.

The spell was broken, and without another word, they turned towards the road. Mannering still had Lorna's arm in his, and was thinking as much about her as the case. He didn't notice the man on the other side of the road, lurking in the shadows. They crossed, stepping out as a car approached. Green Street was only twenty yards or so away from here. There was a large waste patch, where the houses had been rased ; this was now in utter darkness ; darkness which could hide murder.

They neared it.

The man behind them drew closer, and still made no sound. When he drew his knife, he hid the blade up his sleeve. He was only two yards behind, near enough to strike, when they actually reached the corner ; a low wall prevented them from crossing the waste patch. He turned, also. In the distant light of a street lamp, he could see Mannering's figure clearly, and he knew where to strike, knew exactly what thrust was needed to reach the heart.

Two yards . . .

He kicked against a stone.

The noise broke startlingly across the quiet. It burst upon the Mannerings, who were ambling, sharing those troubled thoughts. It made Lorna exclaim, with the alarm that unexpected noises always created; and it made Mannering spin round.

He saw the man, with the raised knife glinting.

" *John!* " screamed Lorna.

The man lunged.

Mannering knew that he couldn't avoid him, could only lessen the viciousness of the blow. He jumped forward. The knife swept down, and cut into his coat sleeve with a slicing movement; the sharp pain hardly counted. He tried to close with the man, who realised that he'd lost his first chance, and swerved to one side, knife raised again. He slashed.

Lorna was in the way.

" Jo——" began Lorna, and then her voice died away.

Mannering could see her face, pallor in the darkness, could even see the glitter in her eyes. She swayed. The man with the knife was racing along the emptiness of Green Street, and Mannering let him go, having no possible choice. Mannering didn't speak, but moved to Lorna. She fell against him, a dead weight.

He felt an awful fear.

" Lorna, where is it ? " he heard himself say. " Where did he hurt you ? "

She didn't answer.

" Where is it ? " he asked savagely, but it was with the savagery of his own helplessness. He raised his voice : " *Help!* " he shouted. " *Police, police!* " Now, Lorna was leaning against him, and his hands were exploring desperately, fearfully. There was no blood at her back, none at her neck, none on her arms.

There was blood at her breast.

" *Police, police!* " he shouted.

She was still a dead weight against him, and would fall if he moved. He did not know what to do; just felt distraught. The suddenness of it, the fact that she had been cut down and might be dead.

"*Fetch the police !* " he cried desperately, but he wanted a doctor, and he wanted to be able to pad whatever wound there was. The numbness of the shock vanished as a man in a small car drew up, and got out nervously. "Get to a telephone, doctor wanted urgently ! " Mannering cried, and the words nearly choked him.

Then he found the wound, on Lorna's left side.

Three-quarters of an hour afterwards he walked out of the hospital in Tite Street, moving stiffly, looking straight ahead at the car park with a few cars dotted about. His own Rolls-Bentley wasn't there, for he'd come with an ambulance.

They were operating, and there wasn't a thing he could do. There was hardly a thing he could feel.

A car came along, swung round into the hospital car park, and drew up at the foot of the steps. A man jumped out, vivid in the light from the main entrance. He was tall, brisk-moving, dressed in pale grey. He saw Mannering and stopped. Mannering looked at him, knew who it was and, without a change of expression, went to meet him.

This was Superintendent Bristow, of New Scotland Yard.

9

BRISTOW OF THE YARD

" THAT'S RIGHT," MANNERING SAID SAVAGELY. " SHE'S
in the theatre now. There isn't a man alive who
can tell me whether she'll ever come round. That's how
bad it is. An hour ago I was telling myself there wasn't
a thing I could do in this job, and now——" He broke
off, swung round, and splashed whisky into a glass.
" Another ? " he barked.

" Mine'll do, thanks." Bristow was very quiet.

Mannering tossed his head back, the drink down.

" As it is now," he went on as if he hadn't paused,
" I'll live it and sleep it. Waking and sleeping, dreaming,
thinking, eating and walking, I'll be after them. This
is *my* case. I don't give a damn what you and every
addle-pated ape of a policeman at the Yard says."

" See what you mean," said Bristow mildly.

Mannering said thinly, chokingly. " And you can
see——" He broke off again. He looked at his half-
empty glass for several seconds, then put it down with
great care. As carefully, he lit a cigarette. All this
time, his expression was unchanging ; had a hardness
but lacked the savagery he had shown a few minutes
before. The glitter had gone out of his eyes, too, and
hardness replaced it. His voice had changed, was flat
and harsh. " All right, Bill. Sorry. What I'm saying
is that I'm going after them with all I've got. You
are, too. Never was a better job to work together."

Bristow was looking at him steadily.

" Yes," he said. " And no. There have been times
when I've wished you in Timbuctoo, anywhere off a
case. This one——" He shrugged. He had square
shoulders, and was nicely tailored. He had rather a
pale face because these days he spent most of his time

in the office. His eyes were pale grey. His features were good, but seemed to lack character; in fact, he didn't. His small, close-clipped moustache would have been iron grey like his smoothly brushed hair, but for the dark stain of nicotine at the centre, paling towards the corners of his lips. "What I mean, John, is that I almost wish they'd got you, too, instead of just your sleeve. Not badly; only enough to make you rest up until you'd got over the bad stage. Because in this mood, you'll probably get yourself killed. That won't help Lorna."

Mannering said: "Straight from the shoulder, eh?"

"That's right."

"Bill," Mannering said, "I saw those two men on the road near Orme. That's the only possible reason for an attack. I know them both. So whatever I do, they're after me. If I sit back and wait for it, they'll have an easier job."

"Don't intend to argue," Bristow said. "When you telephoned, you asked me to tell Aylmer, down at Orme. I did that, and he's sending a man to watch Joanna Woburn. She should be all right."

There was another pause, before Mannering said:

"Under police protection, she 'should' be all right. Touching faith!" Mannering drew at his cigarette and stubbed it out, half-smoked. He sipped his whisky again, then put it down. He looked at the telephone, and although he had been warned that hours would pass before he could hope for news, the longing for it was in his eyes. "Know anything about this, Bill?" he asked abruptly.

Bristow tapped the side of his nose.

"Only what Aylmer told me. I'd warned him that you knew George Merrow, and that you didn't always behave yourself, but that doesn't matter now. What do *you* know? And if you hold anything back——"

"Nothing I knew helped." Mannering told the Yard man about the story of a heavy weight on Jimmy Garfield's conscience for twenty years, and went on:

"Garfield knew that a crisis was coming, but didn't expect it so soon. It came as soon as they got George Merrow out of the way. Merrow's the one man who might be able to tell us something. And Merrow——"

"John," Bristow interrupted, "I can't stop you from trying to find who did it. I don't even know that I want to. I only say that you'll be crazy if you start while you're in this mood. You're half crazy with anger and you're terrified in case Lorna should die. Plan what you like, say what you like, rage as much as you like, but don't *do* anything yet. Cool off."

The telephone bell rang.

Mannering, quite motionless just before the first sound, went to it like a bullet. He had the receiver off the platform as Bristow was turning round. Yet with the earpiece close to his head, he hesitated. Then he said slowly :

"This is John Mannering."

He paused, and relaxed. He pulled up a chair, and dropped on to it. "Yes, I'll hold on," he said, and looked across at Bristow. "It's a call from Orme." He waited without speaking, but fidgeting in his chair. He read Bristow's attitude correctly ; it was a kind of exasperated commiseration. He knew that all that Bristow said was true, the advice was sound, but——

"Hallo, is that Mr. Mannering ? "

"Yes, speaking."

"Miss Woburn would like a word with you, sir," a man said. "Hold on a moment, please."

There was another pause. In it, Mannering pictured the great house, with its grace, its spaciousness and its beauty. He could see the pictures, the tapestries, the suits of armour, the breastplates, the chain mail, the pikes and the huge swords which looked too massive and too heavy for a man to wield.

"Mr. Mannering," Joanna Woburn said, "I just felt that I had to telephone you. I—I've heard about what happened. Is—is there any news of your wife ? "

"No, not yet," Mannering said, and found it easier to

speak than he had expected. "It'll be several hours before I hear. Everything all right down there?"

"Oh, yes, it will be now the police are watching."

Mannering said: "Don't take a thing for granted, Miss Woburn. Watch what you do, where you go, whom you meet. Don't go anywhere alone, don't evade the police, don't be fooled by false messages. You've seen what these people are prepared to do."

"I'll be careful," she said. "I only wish I could help."

"Don't start blaming yourself," Mannering said sharply. She had lifted him out of himself, although he didn't realise it then. "Take care, and——" He paused.

After a moment she said: "Yes?"

"I think it would be a good idea if we had a talk about George Merrow," Mannering said slowly. "To-morrow, some time. Soon, anyhow."

"Why about Mr. Merrow?"

"Would Jimmy Garfield confide in him?"

Joanna confessed: "I just don't know, I'd only be guessing if I said one way or the other." She sounded flat and miserable; and there was nothing surprising about that. "I do hope that——"

She just couldn't finish.

Mannering put the receiver back; and automatically lit another cigarette. He filled in the outline which Bristow had already heard. He felt less restless, and saw Bristow and his arguments more clearly.

He could drink himself into forgetfulness and it wouldn't help. He could take some wild chance that would bring another attack, and if Lorna did recover——

He had to accept the possibility that she might not.

He moved from spot to spot, aware of Bristow's steady gaze, and saying nothing. Tension came into the room, and both men were sharply aware of it.

Bristow broke the silence.

"All right, John," he said. "You're going to feel like this for a long way. Hot and cold. Now I'm going to tell you what *I'm* going to do. One of the best men

I've got will be on your tail every minute from now on. If you slip him, it will be your own fault, and I shan't mourn so much at your funeral. Now for one or two general principles." He gave a quick, unamused smile. "We know they are killers. We know that they plan very carefully. We know that they're daring. We know that they wanted that box of Garfield's desperately enough to kill, plan and take big risks. I don't know of anyone running loose at the moment who fits all those categories, which means that we're probably up against someone we've never come across before. They'll have new tricks, new hide-outs, possibly new methods. That's going to make it tough. They want to be able to move about freely, or it wouldn't matter so much to them that they'd been seen. Whatever they're doing isn't finished yet—if it were, they'd almost certainly have made plans to get out of the country as soon as this job was over." Bristow lit a cigarette from the stub of the one he was smoking, and when it was drawing smoothly, went on in the same level voice : " So when we say we don't know a thing about these people, we actually know a lot. There are some other things you may have forgotten about. We've got the big black Packard, and we're working on that. We know that this Woburn woman fired a shot at a small car, and scored a hit, so somewhere or other there's a little car with a bullet mark in the back. We have the descriptions of the men, which you can give, and while they may not be all that detailed they'll help." He paused again, and then flung out : " Ever taken the trouble to estimate the number of policemen in this country ? "

He looked so aggressive that it cracked Mannering's stiffness.

" No, Bill."

" It runs into a hundred thousand odd. Every one of them is getting ready to go for these people. Don't run away with the idea that if you can't catch 'em, no one can. Now and again, on a highly specialised job, you can pull out that little extra that we haven't got. I'm not sure you can on this. And," added Bristow, moving closer and compelling Mannering to look straight into his eyes, " if that isn't enough, *I* don't want you dead. Will you help us to keep an eye on you ? "

Mannering said : " All right, Bill. Thanks." He was much more himself, and a hint of a smile played at his lips. " Impressive tally you've made, and there's only one thing you've missed."

" What's that ? " Bristow looked taken aback.

" Whatever was in that box, it wasn't miniatures ; at least, not only miniatures," Mannering asserted. " I've been checking. I may have missed a few rare collections, but the box was about twelve inches by fourteen, according to Miss Woburn, and quite flat. Miniatures of any value wouldn't be packed without protection, so there isn't a big collection. The biggest one in the world wouldn't be valuable enough to justify what's happened."

Bristow rubbed his nose. " See what I mean by your specialised knowledge ? "

" There may be half a dozen collections worth a fortune, but not money enough to justify the risks these people take," Mannering went on, as if he wanted to emphasise that reasoning for his own benefit as well as Bristow's. " I suppose it's arguable that Garfield's whole fortune would be worth the gamble—any idea how much he's actually worth ? "

" No." Bristow shrugged. " Millions."

" Two or twenty ? " Mannering asked. " That's something to find out. Do we know whom he'll leave it to, who would have the handling of it when he's dead ? He's seventy now. Would a man of seventy be careless enough to leave no will ? Any will found ? "

" None reported yet," Bristow said. " What do you know about Garfield ? "

" Not much. He used to be a customer of mine, but stopped buying from me about ten years ago. He had an accident, and injured his spine. When he recovered enough to be wheeled about, he went to Brook House, which he'd bought a year before but never lived in. He took in a big staff, mostly local people ; the only one of his old servants was his butler, Gedde. He turned the place into a museum, and seldom left it. He didn't ever come to London, just shut himself up with his hoard."

Bristow asked : " D'you think he has a hoard of stolen goods ? "

" I just don't know," Mannering said evenly.

" *I'm* going to find out," Bristow announced.

" Take a look at other aspects of the set-up," urged Mannering. He wasn't anything like so restless now that his mind was working and probing. " A seventy-year-old man living in a house fit for the Middle Ages, one butler, a housekeeper and several local servants, and a nephew who appeared out of the blue about two months ago—just before Joanna Woburn arrived, I gather. Finally, Joanna herself. There's so much to work on that there's ample room for us both, Bill, whether Jimmy Garfield cut himself off from reputable dealers because of stolen goods or not."

Bristow said slowly : " That sounds more like you. But don't have a relapse." He hesitated. " I must get back to the Yard, there's another job needing a lot of attention. Have you told your friends the Plenders about this yet ? "

" They're in Italy."

" Larraby ? "

" He flew over to Paris for a sale for me, and it'll last a week."

" Not a man with many close friends, are you ? " Bristow remarked. " I don't think you're the right man to be here on your own. Anyone you can think of to call on ? "

" No wet-nurse, thanks," Mannering said, and unexpectedly clapped Bristow on the shoulder. " Sometimes I think you're a better man than the Yard deserves ! Thanks."

Bristow shrugged.

He went out, and Mannering watched him from the front door. Bristow's grey head vanished beneath a

turn in the stairs. His footsteps sounded clearly, gradually getting quieter. Soon, they echoed from the hall,
and a moment afterwards the front door opened and
closed.

Mannering turned back into the flat.

As he closed the door, he knew exactly what Bristow
meant. Its emptiness seemed to strike at him. Fear
of bad news was like the engulfing wave of a boisterous
sea. He fought against the mood and beat it back, but
knew that it would never be far away.

Now, he had to wait.

He looked at the telephone in his study, then pulled
up an armchair and sat down. In his mind's eye there
was a picture of white-coated surgeons and white-clad
nurses, the bright light over Lorna, the flashing of steel,
the quiet.

And somewhere in the sprawling mass of London was
the man who had struck her down, and those whom he
served.

10

MORNING

LUCIEN SEALE SLEPT WITH HIS LEFT HAND ABOVE HIS head, his right beneath the bedclothes. He lay slightly on his left side, giving him freedom of movement. He appeared to sleep very soundly, but a faint click at the door made him open his eyes. Apart from that, he didn't move; but he could see the door.

Someone tapped.

Seale closed his eyes, but looked through his lashes. Like that, he looked even more unreal, like a mummy into which a kind of life had been breathed. His hair was greying and untidy, that was the only human look about him. His nostrils were distended. The light falling upon his face showed some of the tiny marks which were almost inseparable from skin grafting.

The tap came again, more loudly.

He opened his eyes wide, but didn't sit up. A watch ticked at the bedside table. He looked at the handle of the door, and listened intently, hearing only distant sounds, and nothing from the door.

Then whoever was out there in the passage turned and walked away.

Seale relaxed.

He sat up in bed, in a pair of washed-out pyjamas which had once been bright blue. He rubbed his eyes, and then stretched out for the watch; it was half-past seven. He got out of bed. He moved freely enough, it was the deliberation which touched the movements with a kind of artificiality. At the window, he stared into the front garden, saw two cyclists and a bus pass, the morning sun making the bus's red paint look like fresh blood. Then Seale looked across the green quiet of the Heath.

A dog frisked, not far away.

Seale yawned, ran a hand over his face, and went to the door. He didn't trouble to put on a dressing-gown. The legs of the pyjamas were too short for him, and one was torn, so that most of the leg from the knee downwards showed ; it was very white and almost free from hairs. He unlocked the door, opened it, and stepped out. No one was in the passage. He let the door bang and while he was in the bathroom heard Paul Greer running up the stairs.

"Lucien, you there ? "

"Coming," Seale called. He washed his hands and face in cold water, and then went out.

Paul Greer was in grey flannels, a yellow shirt and a red muffler tied choker-fashion. He looked plump, sleek, well-fed and rested.

"I thought you were never going to wake up," he complained. "I tried——"

"I know you tried. It's lucky for you you didn't try to force your way in."

Whatever the shorter man was going to say wasn't uttered. He blinked up at Seale, and then gave an involuntary shiver. He turned and led the way towards the bedroom. Seale took off his pyjama jacket. He was so thin that his ribs showed through, and he had that same whiteness. There were two big, puckered scars, one at his right shoulder and the other just above his stomach.

"You just don't trust anybody, do you ? " Greer said at last.

"Not even you."

"What would I have to gain by double-crossing you ? " asked Greer heavily. "Not a thing, and you know it. You scare me sometimes, you aren't like you used to be."

Seale grinned. "You never said a truer word ! "

"I didn't mean that way," Greer said uneasily. "You know what I mean. You used to be—oh, forget it. I wanted to tell you——"

Seale said : "We don't forget it, Paul, we remember

it." He didn't move; yet he seemed to hold Greer by sheer hypnotic force, so that the plump man couldn't escape. "That's one of the things you have to learn. I don't *ever* forget. I don't forget that I got smashed up the way I did. I don't forget that I had to be given a new face, and some new skin in a lot of other places. I don't forget that it took me five years—five years, Paul—in a hospital, going through agony time after time, before I could show myself in public. No, I don't forget, I'm not made that way. Even if I were, every time I looked into a mirror I'd be reminded of what had happened." He moved towards the wash-basin, and turned on the hot tap, looking hard at his face in the mirror. "There's one thing, I don't have to shave now, do I, Paul? There's another thing: I want what I want and I'm going to get it. If it hadn't been for that old swine at Orme this wouldn't have happened to me. First he double-crossed me, then——"

Greer made himself interrupt. "Listen, Lucien. He didn't know what he was doing, he couldn't have guessed that you'd be smashed up the way you were. Hell, that was an accident."

"It was an accident that wouldn't have happened if he hadn't swindled me," Seale sneered. "But he doesn't matter any more. He left a safe deposit key and the keys to his own vault in that box, we can use both. From now on, I'm on the way up. Don't forget it. I've been as far down as a man can be, and now I'm going as high as a man can go. There are two people in this world who might be able to stop me. One is Mannering, and the other is Joanna Woburn."

"If you'd left the woman to me——"

"But I didn't, did I?" sneered Seale. "I wanted to see what happened myself, and if I hadn't been there probably you and the others would have been caught. That's how good you are." He turned away from the basin. "That's how *good*. What kind of men have you got on the pay roll, Paul? You're supposed to look after that. A man had a simple job to do last night, and what happened ? He misses Mannering and makes him raging mad, makes the job we've got ten times more difficult. That's wonderful, Paul, isn't it ? Brilliant. The——"

Greer said almost desperately : " Why don't you listen to reason ? Mannering isn't going to sit and wait for you to knock him off. He's good. Look at the way he acted yesterday afternoon, look at the way he saved himself last night. He has some luck, but he wouldn't have so much if we weren't good. It's not going to be so easy."

" It's going to be done."

Paul said : " I don't know, Lucien, I just don't know."

" That mean you're scared ? "

Greer gave a funny little explosive laugh. " Too right I'm scared ! Ever since we teamed up again, I've been scared. There's something in you that I don't like. It terrifies me. You're good, but you won't listen to reason. This time, reason says that you ought to lie low for a long time. Maybe you ought to work through a stooge and not show yourself——"

" I don't use any stooge," Seale said. " We get Mannering and the girl, quickly." He began to put on singlet and trunks. " What did you come to see me so early for ? "

There was a long pause. Then :

" Peter's here," Greer answered. " He wants to cross into France and stay there for a few weeks, in case anything went wrong last night. I wouldn't let him until I'd got your okay."

Seale didn't answer.

After a minute, Greer said testily : " He's waiting and I'm waiting, and you don't have to behave as if you were King of the Cocoa Islands."

For some reason, that amused Seale.

" Okay, Paul, okay ! You can tell Pete no, we've got more work for him. Just tell him to lie low in London for a few days ; as soon as we've finished he can find himself a skirt and take her to the Riviera. Just between you and me, he hasn't earned his corn yet."

Greer said: "That's true enough, but if he's scared he might be dangerous."

"Soothe him, Paul," urged Seale. "Don't let him be scared. You know how good you are with men like Pete. Now there's that old police uniform—we still got it?"

"Yes."

"Mannering wouldn't expect trouble from a copper, would he?" Seale asked thoughtfully. "Try that old trick—with a knife. If it doesn't work, we'll use one of those hand-grenades you bought, and throw it into his car."

"But other people might——" began Greer sharply. Seale just showed his teeth, and rasped into the silence: "Nancy up yet?"

"Yes."

"Tell her I want some tea, now, and then some breakfast," Seale ordered. "And over breakfast we can discuss how to kill Mannering and the Woburn girl." He actually chuckled. "Not that there ought to be any difficulty with the Woburn girl, she's sitting right in the heart of trouble, isn't she?"

Greer flashed: "You can't use anyone down there now!"

"Can't I?" asked Seale. "We'll see."

"Listen, you can't risk——"

"Why don't you worry less and do what you're told more?" Seale asked. "When we're ready, we can use who we want. Now we have that box, we have nearly everything. It's just a matter of patience. Go and tell Mickey and Nancy."

Greer shrugged, and went out, obviously uneasy.

Seale put on his rather shabby clothes. He didn't smile, didn't change his expression. He did not speak to the young woman who came in with tea on a tray, not even to answer her "Good-morning, Lucien." She did not seem surprised, but went out at once.

Downstairs, she said to Paul Greer: "He's going to

run himself and a lot of other people into big trouble if we're not careful."

"He'll calm down."

"I'm not so sure." Nancy pushed her heavy corn-coloured hair back. She had big, bold features, a big, rather floppy figure ; she needed corsets, not just a belt. "Know what I think ? I think he's just eaten up with hatred."

"For whom ? " Paul asked. "The old so-and-so at Orme, or——"

"Anyone on two legs," Nancy said.

Mannering woke, slowly.

He felt a pain at the back of his neck and another behind his right knee. For the first few seconds he didn't know why, or where he was ; then he realised that he wasn't in bed, but in an armchair in the study. His mouth was harsh and dry, his eyes were heavy. The whisky bottle was on the table by his side, with his glass and Bristow's.

Bristow's——

He remembered.

He had started to move, but now sat absolutely still. He stared at the whisky bottle ; there was the head and shoulders of a Highlander on it, a ruddy-faced man with blue eyes ; the picture faded, and Mannering seemed to see Lorna, alive—and dead.

He got up, slowly. His neck and his knee still hurt. He stared at the telephone. He had last spoken into it at four o'clock, when the hospital had called to tell him that the operation was over, she was comfortable, there would be no further news until next morning.

It was half-past eight.

He moistened his lips, then went into the empty kitchen and put a kettle on. All he could really think about was telephoning the hospital, but eagerness to do that was touched with fear of what the news might be. He made himself go into the study again, and pick up the receiver. He dialled the hospital number.

" . . . Hospital, can I help you ? "

" Hold on, please."

" I'm trying to find Sister, hold on, please."

Hold on, hold on, hold on.

" Oh, Mr. Mannering, I'm sorry to have kept you."
He knew the Day Sister, and this was her bell-like voice.
" There isn't very much change to report."

Mannering dropped into the chair.

" So she's—kept going ? "

" Yes, steadily," the Sister said briskly, " and the
fact that she has got through the night makes it more
hopeful."

" If I come——"

" You could come, and be thoroughly distressed," the
Day Sister said. " If you stay near a telephone, I'll
make quite sure that you have all the news as it comes
through, and you're only ten minutes' drive away from
the hospital. I should stay home, if I were you." The
briskness softened a little. " Really, I'm most hopeful,
and I know Dr. Morrison is."

" Bless you," Mannering said fervently. " I'll be here,
unless I send a message."

He rang off.

He heard the kettle boiling, but didn't get up.

He was beginning to realise just what it would mean to
him if Lorna didn't recover, and didn't come back. This
flat, with his old furniture, its charm, its picturesqueness,
would seem empty and barren without her. He was
almost maudlin, and knew it, but there wasn't a thing
he could do about it.

That kettle !

He jumped up.

After a bath and shave, he boiled two eggs and made
some toast. It was a bright morning and he sat looking
out of the window of the small dining-room ; he could
see the distant Thames, and a few small craft moving
slowly along it. The newspaper carried a small story
of the attack on him, only one had a picture of Lorna ;
but all his friends would know, now, the telephone would

soon start ringing ; it was surprising that it hadn't started already.

Before he finished breakfast, it began.

Friends, the Press, Bristow, an assistant at Quinns, Ethel with her twisted ankle, came on the line one after another. Anxious, worried, curious. At moments it infuriated him, at others he realised that it was giving him plenty to think about. Into a lull, he sat back and smoked a cigarette—and heard the front-door bell ring.

He was half-way to the door before the possibility dawned on him that this might be danger in a new guise. He stopped, a yard from the door. He couldn't see through it from here, but there was a small spy-hole, put there almost as a joke, a few months ago. He could see through that, if he went close to the door.

The bell rang again.

It might be a policeman ; it might be a friend ; it might and probably was a newspaperman. There wasn't the slightest reason to believe that it might be anyone with intent to kill, yet he couldn't get the thought out of his mind.

The police were watching, weren't they ?

He reached the spy-hole, and peered through. At first all he saw was a patch of blue, and glitter of something silvery. Then the man out there moved back a little, and Mannering saw his helmet, his collar with the Metropolitan police numbers on it.

He relaxed, feeling sharply annoyed with himself. His nervous reaction was partly due to Bristow, he shouldn't be anything like so jittery.

One copper.

He opened the door.

The ' policeman ' held a knife.

11

THE 'POLICEMAN'

HE WAS A SHORTER MAN THAN MANNERING, YOUNG, hard-eyed. The knife was in his right hand, held just in front of him, dagger fashion. He lunged, as soon as the door was open, and the knife should have buried itself in Mannering. Mannering flung himself to one side, felt the blade catch in his coat, and smashed his right fist at the 'policeman's' face. The man backed away, gasping.

Mannering snatched at the wrist above the knife. He felt the other screw himself up for a desperate effort. For a moment they stood together, grunting, straining to get the knife.

Mannering knew that if he failed, he would be killed.

The other man's left hand was at his wrist, twisting, thrusting his arm upwards. Mannering was forcing the man's hand downwards so that the point of the knife was thrust towards the floor. They hardly moved ; just steeled themselves for greater effort. Sweat gathered on their foreheads. If he relaxed, even if he shouted, Mannering knew that the other would have that vital moment that he needed for the kill.

Then Mannering butted the 'policeman' on the nose, and as the man sagged back, twisted the bony wrist. He felt the finger tendons relax, and heard the knife clatter. He struck again, savagely. The 'policeman' staggered away, doubled up with pain, very close to the top of the stairs. He couldn't stop himself, and Mannering couldn't stop him. The 'policeman' fell backwards from the head of the stairs, then thudded down to the first landing.

Mannering stood at the top, breathing very hard.

For a few seconds, nothing happened or moved. Then

he saw that the man was lying very still, and his neck
seemed to be oddly twisted. Slowly, Mannering went
downstairs. Next he heard the street door open, and a
man called up :

"Everything all right there ? "

Mannering drew a deep breath.

"Come—up," he called.

He reached the man who lay in that oddly shaped
heap. He felt quite sure what had happened, it was
plain to see. He couldn't possibly blame himself, but
deep bitterness built up inside him, going as deep as
bitterness and self-reproach could go.

This man was dead.

The man who'd just come in, a Yard man on street
duty, came at the double. He slackened his pace when
he saw the 'policeman', looked into Mannering's bleak
eyes, and started to excuse himself. He had actually
spoken to the man, asked him what Division he'd come
from ; the letters on his uniform had tallied with his
story ; he couldn't be blamed. . . .

"No one's blaming you," Mannering said tautly. "No
one's blaming anybody."

But a man who might have talked was dead.

By the middle of the morning the police were able to
say that the dead man was a Peter Arthur Byall, with a
record for robbery with violence. He had been in France
for some months, and had only just returned to England.
He had rooms at Highgate, where his landlady swore that
she knew nothing about him. He also had a motor-
cycle, and might be the man who had stabbed Lorna.
A call went out for anyone who knew anything about his
movements during the past few weeks, but there was no
response.

"The one inescapable thing is that you can't feel safe
anywhere," Bristow said. "If they really mean to get
you, they can strike from a dozen places and use a dozen
foul tricks." He looked into Mannering's face, badly

shaken because the man he had sent to watch Mannering had fallen down on his job; and because he felt quite sure that Mannering was in acute danger. "After this, I feel quite sure they mean to kill you. Everything else being even, they will."

"Job's comforter," Mannering said. "Two attempts have failed."

"I'm sick and tired of arguing with a pig-headed fool," Bristow rasped. "I know what you *feel*, and I hate having to say what I'm saying. But given a man who is determined to kill you at all costs, there's no way in which we can guarantee your safety. Know what I think you ought to do?"

Mannering said slowly, softly: "Go on."

"If I had my way, you'd be out of the country in a few hours' time."

"You forget——"

"I don't forget Lorna or anything or anyone," Bristow said. "Lorna's still keeping going. The last I heard from the hospital, they were optimistic. You can keep in touch by telephone. But whether you stay in the country or not, you've got to leave this flat, keep away from Quinns, keep under cover."

Mannering just looked at him.

"The same applies to Joanna Woburn," Bristow said. "I'd pack the pair of you off, if——"

"Bill," said Mannering, in a soft, smooth voice, "I think you may have got something. I really do. Lie low. Disappear." He began to smile. "Why not? I needn't leave England, need I? You don't really expect me to, that was just to impress me with the depth of your feeling." He laughed, with a burst of excitement. "I could do two jobs at the same time, Bill, look after Joanna Woburn and probe into the problem of Jimmy Garfield. Be useful to know who'll inherit if he dies. Found his will yet?"

"No."

"Who are his solicitors?"

"Hodderburn, White and Hodderburn, of Lincoln's

Inn," Bristow said. " They've been handling his legal affairs for seven or eight years. Know them ? "

" I believe I know the junior Hodderburn," said Mannering. " I think he might be prepared to play ball, too." He looked and felt almost excited as he moved about the flat. " Supposing I turn myself into a lawyer, Bill, and go down to look after Garfield's interests while he's on the danger list and George Merrow's *hors de combat* ? "

Bristow didn't speak.

" And we could tell the world or the newspapers that I've had to go abroad, or been warned off by the cops," said Mannering. Gaiety was back in his eyes ; for a few moments, he felt as if all the fear had gone, all the frustrations were over. The mood would soon go, but he would probably never be in the same slough of despond. " Bless your old heart, you've scored a bull. Exit, John Mannering. Enter, a junior Hodderburn ! I needn't be one of the family, of course, provided I'm one of the firm." He actually chuckled, as if delighted. " How does it strike you ? "

" In anyone else, I'd say you were crazy," Bristow said, heavily. " In you——"

They didn't speak.

The years that they had known each other seemed to come between them, with all the things they knew about each other. Mannering was quite sure of the trend of Bristow's thoughts, could imagine how the irony of the situation affected him. But Bristow would have only one purpose ; to help him, and get to the heart of the matter.

" John," Bristow said at last, " Joanna Woburn knows you, Aylmer knows you, several of the police down there saw you the other morning. They're mostly trained observers. I don't think you'd get away with a disguise."

" Don't you ? " asked Mannering softly. " Don't you, Bill ? "

" No."

" I think we'll put it to the test," Mannering said.

"Will you have a word with Hodderburn, White and Hodderburn and tell them how highly respectable you think I am?" He couldn't repress a chuckle. "Of course, you're taking a lot of risks, for Brook House is full of priceless treasures. I might stage the biggest ever robbery, and get away with it. Who knows?"

Bristow said: "First, you have to get under cover. We can think about this crazy idea afterwards."

"Bill," declared Mannering firmly, "it's a deal. If you won't fix it with the solicitors, I'll find a way—with them, with an insurance company, with someone who knows Garfield. I'll be near Joanna. They'll probably have a cut at her, and——" He didn't finish. "You can see how well it would work as well as I can."

"No man can disguise himself so well that he can't be recognised," Bristow objected.

"Bill," said Mannering again, "I'll talk to you, face to face as now, and you'll never know it."

William Bristow drove more slowly than usual towards Scotland Yard and, when he reached it, sat at the wheel for a few minutes before getting out.

He was in the middle fifties, not so springy as he had been, and looking very grim, almost dour. He had a problem and he didn't know anyone who could share it with him, or make it any lighter.

In the past few years, there had been many retirements and not a few changes at the Yard. He was one of the old brigade. He was, in fact, the only man now on the staff of the Criminal Investigation Department who knew beyond any shadow of doubt that John Mannering was the Baron.

He was one of the few who remembered the days of the Baron vividly. He had cause to. As a comparatively new Inspector, he had first clashed with the jewel-thief who had taken London by storm. Looking back, it was easy to see it in terms of melodrama; and no one who had not lived through the period would quite believe how sensational they had been. Yet here at the Yard, in the files, was a dossier of the Baron, with newspaper cuttings by the thousand. Bristow didn't need to refer to the dossier ; he knew it all by heart. He could picture the huge headlines, in inch-high letters of black :

BARON ESCAPES AGAIN

THE BARON—RAFFLES OR ROBIN HOOD ?

They were just samples ; the kind of thing one would find in the children's comics of the day, but there had been nothing comical. Paris had suffered the Baron, too, and other capital cities in Europe. They called him jewel-thief extraordinary, and forgot—and it was easy to forget—that he had started just as an ordinary thief, out of the bitterness of a broken romance.

It was easy for Bristow to forget that, too.

It was much simpler to remember the later days, when the bitterness had worn itself out. Then, the public sense of adventure and excitement had been very strong, for the Baron had sought out men of great wealth and robbed them, ruthlessly—and given the proceeds to the poor.

That had gone on for years.

The Baron had been front-page news longer than any man on the wanted list whom Bristow remembered. He'd won the admiration and eventually even the plaudits of a host of people, the good and the bad, and then, he had vanished from the scene.

Soon afterwards, John Mannering, a wealthy man-about-town renowned for his knowledge of precious stones and *objets d'art*, had bought Quinns.

Very few had suspected, and only Bristow had been quite sure, that Mannering and the Baron were one and the same. Bristow had lacked proof. He could think back over the dozens of times when he had worked desperately to find it, when his liking for Mannering had clashed sharply with his Yard's attitude towards the Baron. He had never had to put friendship to the final test ; for once he owned Quinns, Mannering stopped working as the Baron; but there were many things he had learned as the Baron, which served him and others well.

Gradually, his reputation had grown as a private detective. He was occasionally consulted by Scotland Yard, because of his specialist knowledge. He had influence and contacts which spread through the East and the West Ends, and probably no man had a better rubbing acquaintance with fences.

Now, he proposed to disguise himself and go to the home of a millionaire which was spilling over with *objets d'art*, antiques and precious stones. Bristow knew that the poacher had turned gamekeeper, but could never be absolutely sure that the gamekeeper wouldn't fall for the temptation of poaching now and again.

This would be thrusting temptation at him.

Whether the Yard gave its blessing or not, Mannering would do what he planned. As the Baron he had specialised in disguises, and everything he had said to Bristow was true; this was the logical thing for him to do.

No one must know, except the solicitors. Ethel, the Mannerings' maid, was away. Lorna would be in hospital for weeks. No one else *need* know, except——

Bristow reached his office, lit a cigarette, sat down heavily and looked at the blue sky through the open window. His Chief Inspector wasn't in, and the only sound came from the Embankment and the river.

" Oh, let him have a go," Bristow said abruptly. " I'll sell the idea to the A.C., if he says okay, it's okay."

He jumped up.

He checked the impulse to go along to the Assistant Commissioner's office immediately; he wanted more briefing. Reports by the dozen were on his desk and he read through each, first hopefully, then glumly. The whole of London and the Home Counties had been alerted for the men whom Mannering and Joanna had seen.

Finished, Bristow went to see the A.C., who did not know that Mannering and the Baron were one and the same, and who had none of Bristow's qualms.

" Yes, good idea, I'd say. If he's prepared to risk it and Hodderburns will play, go ahead. Try them, and let me know, will you ? "

" Right, sir." Bristow was brisk. " If it comes off, only you and I should know. The fewer the better."

" Well, I suppose we can be trusted not to let anything slip," the A.C. said. He chuckled. Obviously he really thought it a good idea. He didn't dream of Bristow's reservations, knew nothing of what Bristow knew might be an almost unbearable temptation to the man who had been the Baron.

12

THE BARON RE-BORN

AT HALF-PAST ONE THAT DAY, MANNERING HAD A LUNCH brought in by the Yard man now on duty in Green Street; another was on duty at the back.

At a quarter-past two, Mannering telephoned the hospital again; for the first time, he put down the receiver feeling that the deepest of the anxieties was really over.

"She is really doing very well," the Day Sister had said. "By tomorrow, I think you'll be able to see her, but not for very long."

"That's fine," Mannering had answered. "That's wonderful."

He put down the receiver, and went to the window, and looked at the distant Thames; it was shimmering; and his eyes were glistening, too. He turned away at last, but didn't go out.

During the afternoon, Bristow telephoned, was carefully formal, said that the project had the approval of the Assistant Commissioner and the co-operation of Hodderburn, White and Hodderburn. It was thought by the solicitors, Bristow said, that he had better go to Brook House as a private inquiry agent, ostensibly employed by them to try to find why Garfield had been attacked, not as a member of the firm. That would give him a freer hand.

"It's building up nicely," Mannering agreed. "Tomorrow I'm going to see Lorna, and straight after that——"

It was easier to chuckle, now.

Lorna was unconscious, sleeping under a drug. Mannering wasn't surprised by her pallor, and as he looked down at her, he was conscious only of one feeling; a gratitude that it had not been fatal.

He left the hospital about half-past three, and two Yard men followed him. He did not know whether anyone else did. Certainly there was no one whom he recognised.

Yet he felt a keen sense of danger.

He told himself that it was imagination, that because of what he knew, he fancied things which just weren't there. He couldn't be sure. The Yard men, one in a taxi and one in a private car, followed his Rolls-Bentley. He had seldom felt more conspicuous. He drove to Hart Row, and parked the car at a bombed site where he had a special lot. One Yard man got out of the taxi near him, the other parked close by his side.

If he were attacked again, it would be easy to convince his assailants that he had been hurt.

Would he be attacked?

He took it for granted as he walked along Hart Row.

It was warm, yet he felt shivery. The small shops here were all exclusive, and few of the windows had more than half a dozen creations in. One, opposite Quinns itself, was a milliners in which two ostrich feathers, shaped into a bowl, was in solitary glory.

In the window at Quinns was a tiny jewelled crown, blazing with splendour which made even Mannering stop to look. Other people were looking, too, several women gazed in rapt silence.

Mannering didn't go in.

He would be expected here. If anything were to happen, surely it would be at the approach to Quinns— now or later, as he came out. He had that cold, shivery feeling. He was very conscious of the watchful Yard men, one of them looking towards the end of the street, one of them looking up.

Mannering glanced up, too.

The Yard man shouted: "*Look out!*" as if death were falling from the skies.

Women turned round, in alarm, a man glared. Mannering saw a little black ball coming down from the front window two floors above the hat shop. The Yard man seemed to have gone mad, was thrusting the women away, bellowing at them, actually kicking at a man who tried to stop him. Mannering opened the door of the shop, and shouted:

" *In here !* "

Two of the women, terrified, were running wildly towards the end of the street. Two others were jammed in the open doorway of Quinns. Mannering thrust them in and then plunged forward. Then the Yard man did a crazy thing—caught the little black thing, and hurled it away.

It struck a lamp-post, and exploded in mid-air. Pieces of hot metal flew through the air, and Mannering flung up his arms and ' collapsed '.

In fact, he wasn't hurt.

Mannering sat in a small room in a hotel behind the Strand. It was dark outside, but very bright in the room, with specially powerful lamps. At the dressing-table was an elaborate make-up case, open and ready for use. Spread out on the bed were the clothes he would need, and a suit-case ready for packing. His wallet was tight with one-pound notes and he had a reserve supply in the case.

It was nine o'clock.

He was reading the evening papers, and each one did him proud.

MANNERING INJURED IN EXPLOSION
BOMB FELLS JOHN MANNERING
BOMB ATTACK ON FAMOUS JEWELLER

The stories were varied and highly coloured, and the reading public would assume that it had been an attempt at robbery. The only thing in which all accounts tallied was the courage of the Yard man, Detective Sergeant Broad, and the fact that ' only John Mannering was injured and he is now lying dangerously ill in a London Nursing Home '.

No one had been caught.

Bristow had told Mannering, by telephone, that the man throwing the grenade had walked into the offices above the hat shop only ten minutes before Mannering had arrived at Quinns; the two people who had seen him couldn't describe him clearly; they did know that he had had a beard.

He had run away during the confusion.

Mannering put the papers down.

He went to the dressing-table, sat at the stool, and adjusted a table light; it shone pitilessly on him. He stripped to the waist, and as he began to work, his muscles rippled, and his movements had the flexibility which Joanna Woburn had been quick to notice.

Gradually, his complexion changed, becoming more florid. Gradually, the shape of his eyes seemed to alter, and his face looked fuller. He worked with a single mindedness which nothing interrupted. A touch of stain here worked in with great care, one which only a strong spirit and detergent could remove; a lotion which dried the skin at the corners of his eyes and his lips, and gave them a wrinkled look.

All of these things he did with inordinate care.

A different man appeared to be gazing at him from the mirror.

He eased his shoulders, after a while, then picked up a small wing mirror and held it so that he could examine the sides of his face and the back of his neck. He had been to a barber, before coming here, and his hair was cut very close, so close that only the faintest suggestion of a crink appeared in it.

Now, he combed and brushed in a dye which made it look iron grey.

He slipped two cheek pads, kept in place by suction, into position, and at once his cheeks looked much plumper. Then he worked some thin plastic over his teeth, hiding their whiteness, giving them a yellowish look and altering their appearance completely.

Next, he went into the private bathroom, and washed

thoroughly. He examined himself afterwards with close scrutiny. The disguise hadn't shifted at all.

Next, he put on the clothes.

They had been specially made, years ago, by a little tailor who had had good reason to be grateful to the Baron. They were loose fitting, and cunningly cut to alter the shape of his shoulders, to give him inches more round the waist, and make it look as if he were stooping. He had complete freedom of movement, but a man in the middle-fifties, not the early forties, stared at himself in the mirror.

He began to smile as he worked his lips about to make sure that the lines stayed on, and none of the disguise wanted patching.

It didn't.

He put on a pair of brown shoes, which had been heavily mended, and had crepe rubber heels ; they didn't make a sound, and made his feet look sizes larger than they were. He spread his toes in these, as comfortably as in any ordinary pair.

Now, he felt ready.

He left the hotel a little after eleven o'clock, when a night porter who already looked tired asked if he were coming back soon.

" No idea," Mannering said, " if I don't I'll send for my case."

" Very good, sir."

Mannering went out, and towards the Strand. It was pleasantly cool. The noise was all from the West End, there was very little traffic in the Strand when he reached it. He walked briskly, practising a different kind of walk, with his head thrust forward a little. Walk, carriage, voice and mannerisms could all give him away, and it was a long time since he had been forced to live a part as he would be forced to live this.

He reached Trafalgar Square.

Ten minutes later, he waited in the main hall of Scotland Yard, for Bristow ; he had sent in the name of Richardson, which would mean nothing at all to the Yard man.

4

He was kept waiting for ten minutes, then a bulky sergeant came along and said:

"Mr. Bristow can spare you five minutes, if you'll come this way."

"Ta," Mannering said, and walked slowly, to the sergeant's obvious impatience. He was taken to one of the waiting-rooms. The sergeant looked bored, Mannering studied some photographs of sporting triumphs of men of the Yard, then lit a cigarette.

The door opened, and Bristow came in.

The man you knew well often behaved like a different person with a stranger. This would show.

If Bristow suspected the truth about this 'stranger', he didn't reveal it. He looked tired, but his manner was friendly; Bristow wasn't the bullying type.

"Now what can I do for you, Mr. Richardson?"

"As a matter of fact, Mr. Bristow," Mannering said in a voice which was not remotely like his own, "I've got a bit of info. for you, that I think you'll be glad about."

Bristow said almost wearily: "So it's a squeal."

"You can call it a squeal or you can call it what you like," Mannering said. He looked straight into Bristow's eyes; less than four feet separated them, beneath a searching light. "It's about the Mile End Road job, last week. You know, when the kid was croaked. I don't hold with violence, and I don't want anything for my trouble, either. You interested?"

The tiredness faded from Bristow's eyes. The sergeant was no longer bored, but had his notebook out and pencil at the ready.

"Yes, very," Bristow said. "Let's have it."

Mannering said: "You ought to look for a man with red hair, Mr. Bristow. I've got a hot tip, that a man with red hair was taking a good dekko at that shop on the afternoon of the burglary. Then when he broke in the kid woke up, and you know what happened. Red hair, that's the info. You know about that?"

Bristow slid neatly out of that question.

" We'll check. Where did you get the information from, Mr. Richardson ? "

" That's my business," Mannering retorted, almost truculently. " The thing is, it's right. And I don't hold with violence, especially against a kid of nine years of age. Mind you, they shouldn't ever have let him stay alone in the house, but you know how it is." He stood up. " That's the lot, Mr. Bristow, thanks for listening."

" Have you got Mr. Richardson's name and address ? " Bristow asked the sergeant.

" They have in the hall, sir."

" Good." Bristow put out a hand. " We'll check this at once, and be in touch with you if anything develops," he said crisply. " And we'll treat it as confidential, you can rely on that."

" Oh, I can trust *you*," Mannering said. " Can't say that about every ruddy rozzer, but even a bad tree has some good apples ! " He grinned.

Bristow saw him as far as the hall.

Mannering went off, and the Yard sent no one after him. He took a taxi to Victoria Station and then walked to a lock-up garage where, for years, he had kept a reserve car which not even the police knew about, and some tools and a gun and ammunition. He fitted the tools, in a specially made band, round his waist, checked that the automatic was loaded, and slipped it into his pocket.

He left the car in the garage, locked up, and took a bus along Victoria Street, getting off near the Cathedral. Bristow lived in a big block of flats near by. Mannering waited, went up in the lift, rang the Bristows' bell. He knew Bristow's wife, a tall, pleasant woman. She answered the door, and obviously thought that she was looking at a stranger.

" Is Mr. Bristow in, please ? "

" No, he's not, but I'm expecting him any minute," she said. But she didn't ask him in. " You aren't likely to keep him long, are you ? " That came anxiously.

" Five minutes, ma'am," Mannering assured her.

He was waiting in a small room off the lounge when Bristow arrived. Bristow's footsteps were flagging, he was probably feeling his age. It was well after midnight, and he had almost certainly been at the job since eight o'clock that morning.

" I didn't know whether I ought to have told him to come back in the morning or not," Mrs. Bristow said worriedly. " I never *do* know what's the right thing to do. He said five minutes, so I suppose it won't be more than a quarter of an hour."

" Five minutes is the absolute limit," Bristow grunted. " Pop a kettle on while I see him. What name did he give ? "

" Gregory."

Bristow came into the small room. At sight of ' Richardson ', he actually stopped moving. Bewilderment, then sharp annoyance, crossed his face.

" Now, what's this nonsense about ? Are you——".

" No nonsense," Mannering said in his normal speaking voice. " The red-haired man's true, Bill, too. Think I'll do ? "

Bristow didn't answer, just moved to a chair and sat down. He was like that for a long time before he began to smile.

It was nearly ten minutes later, when Mannering was leaving, that Bristow thought belatedly to say :

" Before I pass you out, I'd like to see you in daylight."

" Come to Brook House tomorrow," Mannering invited. " Meanwhile, tell Aylmer and the police down there that Mr. Richardson has your blessing, and they're safe to co-operate with him, will you ? "

" I suppose I'd better," Bristow said, almost grudgingly.

13

BROOK HOUSE

JOANNA WOBURN THOUGHT: "I DON'T KNOW WHETHER I'm going to like him or not."

The fact that a representative from Jimmy Garfield's solicitors was coming had preoccupied her a great deal since the previous afternoon, when Aylmer had told her. From the time she had returned from the encounter on the road, she had been edgy and harassed, but fighting to keep up outward appearances. She was conscious of a sense of strain with everyone, from Aylmer downwards. The fact that the police were seriously worried about the possibility of physical attack didn't help. When she had heard of the injury to Mannering's wife, she hadn't been able to rest until she'd spoken to him.

She wished he was here.

Now, she looked into his brownish eyes, with the pupils enlarged with drops so that the brown colour looked opaque, and didn't know whether to be pleased or sorry. At least, he wasn't a policeman. He was older than she expected, but it was easy to believe that he would be useful in an emergency. Aylmer had told her that there would be a policeman on duty, as well as ' Mr. Richardson, from Hodderburn's '; the policeman was a youthful, quiet-moving detective named White, who had taken over Gedde's position.

Everything worked surprisingly smoothly. Mrs. Baddelow and Priscilla went about their work with the usual efficiency. The girl seemed very subdued. The other servants were doing their normal jobs. White was as self-effacing as Gedde had been, and had none of the faint hint of menace that Gedde had carried.

The news from the hospital could have been much worse. Jimmy Garfield was alive, and had had odd moments of consciousness, while George Merrow's leg was on the mend. It would be a long time before it would be out of the plaster, but the risk of complications seemed to have gone.

Now, there was Richardson.

The newcomer arrived in the middle of the afternoon, in a pre-war Austin, which somehow seemed right for him. He drove himself. His luggage consisted of one suitcase and a handcase, and his clothes were anything but smart ; good, but not smart. He looked rather as if he had been stored away in the solicitors' offices until such an emergency as this, and had been given a good dusting and shaking out, and delivered safely. His rather dry voice wasn't unpleasant, and he had a way of smiling with a touch of drollness. It was almost a mannerism. She wasn't likely to make a friend, but he brought a welcome sense of security ; while he was here from Hodderburn's, she felt that someone represented Jimmy.

" I'll get White to show you round," she said ; " I know you'll forgive me, but I have to go into Orme for an hour."

" Orme," said Mannering, and pursed his lips. " May I ask why ? "

If he were going to question all her movements, he would be as bad as Aylmer ; at least the police just accepted whatever she said, didn't question it.

" I want to see Mr. Merrow."

" Oh, yes," said Mannering. " Mr. Garfield's nephew. I understand that the police guard you wherever you go, Miss Woburn." The little smile came. " Do they do that satisfactorily ? "

" Very," she said dryly.

" Excellent ! Some are expendable, but you——" In a man fifteen years younger, she would have thought that almost fresh. In him, it was gallant. " May I make an alternative suggestion ? I would like to get to know Orme. I will go ahead of you, and we can both be afforded police—ah—protection, and when you have finished with Mr. Merrow, I will be able to spend a few minutes with him." He shrugged deprecatingly. "As one of my tasks."

"It should work out very well," said Joanna.

She told White, who made it easy. At half-past four, when she left, Mr. Richardson's car led the way, she followed in the runabout, which had been repaired, and a police officer followed not far behind. She was not as nervous as she had been ; the other two men gave her a sense of security which she knew was probably false, but which helped.

At heart, she didn't quite believe that the danger was as acute as the others said. Even the attack on Mannering and its consequences had affected her only at the time. To be driving along the quiet country road, through the young trees, past the fields of late hay, or grass or the ploughed fields which had already yielded their harvest, and to think that death might strike, was unbelievable.

Only at quiet moments, usually in the darkness of the night, did fear attack her.

Now, the sun shone.

She saw the square back of the old Austin as well as the nose of the modern police car in the driving-mirror. There had been rain during the night, and the country-side was as fresh as it could be, and sweetly smelling.

She drove fast.

A man outside the parking place of the 'Grey Mare' was hosing down a small blue car, and Jeff Liddicombe, in his shirt sleeves, was talking to him. A huge Alsatian dog stood looking on, ears cocked. Jeff raised a hand in greeting, and Joanna smiled back. It was hard to believe that Liddicombe was Priscilla's father ; he was a big man, running to fat, and without any hint of daintiness ; the only similarity was the fair hair.

It was Priscilla's afternoon off, and she would probably be in Orme. With a boy-friend ? Joanna felt a sharp twinge of an emotion she didn't then recognise, because that made her think of the girl's story.

She hadn't seen George Merrow since the accident.

She had sent a message and some flowers; how could she have done less? She wasn't sure whether she wanted to see him again. What had happened would leave its mark for a long time. One moment, slapping his face for a gratuitous insult; the next freeing him from that ugly trap.

She forgot the danger, forgot the police, even noticed Mr. Richardson only vaguely. She knew the hospital, and pulled up in the main approach. The police car swung off the road and stopped just behind her; the man wouldn't leave her alone anywhere.

She felt a twinge of annoyance.

Richardson had driven on, and she knew that he was due to come here at half-past five; it was now five. George Merrow was in a private ward where visiting hours were elastic. She was still thinking mostly of Merrow. She wasn't going to enjoy the first few minutes of the encounter, and if he appeared to feel any embarrassment, she wouldn't stay more than a few minutes.

The porter directed her to the third floor.

A nurse directed her to Ward 23.

She tapped, and George Merrow called out: " Come in."

Her fingers tightened on the handle, and she hesitated before pushing the door open; she did that more sharply than she intended, and it banged back against the wall. That made her go red, and couldn't have been a worse start. Vexedly, she closed the door and then approached him. She knew that whatever else, she wasn't going to be embarrassed for long. He wasn't going to allow her to, either. He looked pale, but not really ill. There was a cage over his leg, covered by the bedclothes He was grinning at her, and had both arms stretched out, as if to clutch and to hold her to him. For a moment, she hesitated and drew back; then she laughed.

Merrow dropped his arms and chuckled.

" Thanks, Joanna! For that and for coming. But what have I done? No more flowers? "

" I'm having some fruit sent in."

" Cold-hearted wench," said Merrow, while his eyes laughed at her. Her heart beat very fast. " What good to me is Joanna at second-hand ? Sit down, relax, and say anything you like except order me to open my mouth. I do not like nurses."

Before she could stop it, the retort was out :

" That's hardly in character, is it ? "

He started, the smile vanishing ; but it came back quickly, and was in his eyes as well as at his lips.

" Never have I asked for anything more than I asked for that. It isn't their sex I object to, it's their horrid efficiency and the unrelenting starched white uniforms. Not that I'm complaining, mine is a very nice girl. Outsize, in fact, and motherly ! "

Joanna sat at a chair pulled up by the side of the bed, and he took her hand.

They were silent for a long time, and then : " How is it, Jo ? Bad ? "

She was frank. " Sometimes, very," she said.

" What a hell of a thing to have walked into ! "

" I don't suppose either of us expected it." She freed her hand.

" No, I suppose not," agreed Merrow. " Well, no use talking about it now. I've just had a word with the Cutter-Upper-in-Chief, and he says that my venerated Uncle is showing a resistance to Demon Death which would shame a man half his age. He had a conscious and also lucid interval half an hour ago. Like to know what he said ? "

She could picture Jimmy, with his battered head.

" I—well, yes, what did he say ? "

" ' Before this is over,' said he, ' I'll show 'em ! ' "

Joanna's laugh came spontaneously again.

" He's rather wonderful," she said ; " I think I've thought that from the beginning."

" Everything in the garden would have been lovely but for his snake-in-the-grass of a nephew," observed George Merrow. He squeezed her hand again, but didn't hold it too long. " I always believe in talking about the inescapable, it might hurt a bit but the risk of putrefaction gets less. Aylmer has asked me seven hundred and thirty-nine questions, plus the one about what was I doing with that pretty maid when someone took a pot shot at me in the copse."

Joanna said: " There's no need——"

" There's every need. I told him that there was such a thing as a normal man's reaction, and I was caught between an ice box and a fiery furnace, so to speak. I say it in no mood of reproach, Joanna, but do you know how persistently unfriendly you were to me ? Almost as if you suspected from the word ' go ' that I was a revolting young man with unwholesome notions, and——"

" George," Joanna said, very quietly and steadily, " Priscilla put it *very* clearly when she asked : ' What harm is there in a cuddle ? ' " That actually made Merrow wince. " Apart from that, why should I criticise you ? I've no right——"

" That's enough of that one," George said, more roughly. His grip was tight, and almost painful ; he wouldn't look away from her, so she couldn't avoid his eyes. " From the moment you walked into the library, and Jimmy told me who you were, I scented trouble," he declared. " It isn't over yet. You know as well as I do that it's been damned uncomfortable living together on terms of frigid politeness melted only by Jimmy's garrulous chatter. No doubt you thought that I looked at you with thoughts which were not proper. And so I did. I liked your face, your figure, your voice and the way you did your hair. If you'd like it in words of four letters, I fell in love with you. I am still in love with you. And—I resent it."

He didn't smile at that, but uttered the words fiercely. She felt as if her heart had almost stopped beating. With the glitter in his eyes, and fierceness in his manner, he was magnificent-looking.

" I don't want to be in love," he said. " I don't want it to matter a tinker's damn what you think about me. But it did, does and will. Understand ? "

She was flaming red.

" But, George——"

" I don't want any ' but, Georges ', either," he said, and suddenly his fingers were tight about her wrists and he was drawing her forward with surprising strength, although he couldn't move his body freely ; the force came from his shoulders. " *This* is what I want."

He kissed her.

The door opened.

" Oh, dear," said ' Mr. Richardson ', in a tone of dry embarrassment. " Apparently I am a little ahead of my time. Never mind, never mind, I can wait."

14

"AND WHO THE HELL IS THAT?" DEMANDED GEORGE Merrow, as the door closed.

Mannering heard him clearly, for he did not quite close the door. It appeared to be closed, but he stood near it, and heard not only Merrow's question but his heavy breathing; and also the almost agitated breathing of the girl.

"Know him?" Merrow demanded.

"I—he's staying at the house," Joanna said.

"At *Brook* House?"

"Yes."

"Sling him out!"

"He's from the solicitors," Joanna said. A chair scraped. "You can't behave with everyone like that, he happened to look in at an awkward moment, that's all."

Mannering waited——

There was roughness in Merrow's voice: "Awkward for you?" he demanded.

The breathing seemed to get more agitated; the chair scraped again. Silence was almost painful before the woman said quietly and cuttingly:

"There are times when I think you're the rudest man I've ever met. I'm sorry it's turned out like this, but——"

Quick footsteps——

"Jo!" exclaimed Merrow.

Mannering wished he could see inside, but listening had to be enough. He did not think that either of the others realised that he could hear so clearly. He thought that he had interrupted an intensely personal scene, and the little he had heard before he had opened the door made him feel quite sure. Now, he believed that whatever else might be true of George Merrow, he put his heart into that cry of : " Jo ! "

Would the girl ignore or heed him ?

There was a pause, as of uncertainty ; then she spoke in a different, rather tired voice.

" I think we're both overwrought, George. Can't we just talk about ordinary things, and forget——"

" We can talk about what you like, but I can't forget what I'd rather talk about," Merrow said. The edge had gone from his voice, and the way he now spoke was likeable. " All right, Jo. I'm much too tense and taut, and I know it. Blame my adventurous past. What's this about Hodderburn's sending a spy."

" Don't be silly. They thought that with you and Jimmy away——"

" They thought that with Jimmy away," corrected Merrow, " it would be wise not to trust the nephew who appeared out of the blue. Give them full marks for doing their job properly. Mind you, so they should, there must be a quarter of a million pounds' worth of rococo bric-à-brac in the house. You sit on money, lean against money, read money, are reflected in money, sleep with money, breathe money and we're probably going to celebrate Jimmy's next birthday by eating off gold plate. He is negotiating for some."

" No ! "

" Yes," mimicked Merrow. " So Hodderburn's were quite right. But if that sawney-voiced old solicitor's clerk makes himself too much of a nuisance, I shall punch him on the nose."

Mannering heard Joanna's half-reluctant laughter.

" He's not," she said.

" Not what ? "

" A solicitor's clerk."

" What is he ? "

" A private inquiry agent," said Joanna. " He——" She paused again, and Mannering sensed the sudden change in her mood, and in the atmosphere. " George, what——"

He said roughly : " Forget it. I don't like amateur policemen, and I don't know that we want one at the house. But I'm not in a position to do much about it. If he makes a pest of himself, tell me—we'll do something about it then. And you might let me know the kind of question he asks, it would be interesting." Another pause. " Jo, bring your chair a bit nearer."

" No ! " She said that more vigorously than she intended. " I must go, and Mr. Richardson wants to have a word with you. *No !* " she repeated, but the word was smothered, and the chair scraped.

By the time she opened the door and entered the passage, Mannering was at a window, yards away. When he looked round, Joanna was still flushed, and that certainly hadn't lasted from the time he had looked in. He smiled amiably, and promised that he wouldn't be long, then went into the ward.

George Merrow was leaning back on his pillows, almost flat on his back. He looked as if he were in some kind of pain ; and probably his leg hurt. His fists were clenched on the bedspread. He stared at the ceiling, not at the door, and Mannering doubted whether he knew that it had opened again. There was never likely to be a worse time to try to get information out of Jimmy Garfield's nephew. Mannering almost decided not to try, but changed his mind and went forward firmly, looking rather big and ungainly.

He cleared his throat.

" Can you spare me a minute or two, Mr. Merrow ? "

Merrow looked at him, but didn't move otherwise, and didn't answer. The film of sweat on his forehead might be the result of physical pain, or of nervous tension. His face was slightly distorted, but that didn't hide the fact that he was aggressively good-looking.

Then he said harshly : " If I have to. What's it about ? *I'm* not thinking of robbing my uncle of his fortune or his secretary of her——"

" What an unpleasant young man you can be," interrupted Mannering, with the dry matter-of-factness permitted to middle age. Perhaps it was that which stifled Merrow's angry retort; perhaps it was his rider: " Calculated, I suppose, to rebuff any young woman, no matter how well disposed she may be."

" Mind your own damned business ! "

Mannering gave the little smile he had assiduously practised until it came almost naturally.

" But I am not paid to mind my own business, Mr. Merrow, I am paid to mind your uncle's. These attacks upon you——"

" I've said all I'm going to to the police," Merrow told him acidly.

" They are not particularly impressed by your unready tongue," murmured Mannering. " I understand that you have told them that you have no idea why you should have been attacked, although since you lived at Brook House you have been, on several occasions. The obvious conclusion is that you were attacked in order to make the way clear for another assault upon your uncle. Do you subscribe to that ? "

Merrow said : " You can guess."

" Why didn't you tell the police of your danger ? "

Merrow drew a deep breath, but something in the calmness of Mannering's eyes checked an outburst ; he cooled down enough to speak gruffly, and with an answering gleam in his own eyes.

" You haven't judged me aright," he said. " I'm such a gentlemanly nephew, and so considerate for all other people's feelings, that I preferred to hug the secret to my manly bosom rather than to worry Uncle Jimmy."

" Did you know that he was in danger ? "

Merrow snapped : " Damn you, no ! I've told the police——"

" What worries us all is what you haven't told the police. It will worry you, too, if they decide to detain you when you're fit enough to leave." Mannering let that sink in, but it didn't appear to make much impression. " Let's assume that you didn't tell your uncle because you thought it would worry him. Let's assume you didn't believe that he was in any danger. What did you think was the reason for the attacks on you ? " Merrow tightened his lips, looking as if he were clenching his teeth, while Mannering went on in the same calm voice : " What had you done, to deserve being shot at ? "

Merrow didn't answer.

" The police aren't fools," Mannering persisted with calm assurance. " In many years of experience, I've come to admire the way they work, Mr. Merrow. Aylmer is astute, and in this case he is constantly in touch with Scotland Yard. When the Yard gets its teeth into a job, it doesn't let go. The Yard is now probing into your past. It doesn't know much yet, only that you have lived abroad for some years, according to your own statement, and came here, presumably at Mr. Garfield's invitation. That was a little over two months ago, and you were introduced as his nephew."

Merrow still didn't speak.

" Are you his nephew ? " Mannering asked mildly. " The police have their doubts, you know."

Merrow said : " They can doubt, you can doubt, the whole world can doubt. I'm Jimmy Garfield's nephew, and can prove it. As you and the police are so damned clever, go and see Rackley's, the Detective Agency in the Strand. They found me. Jimmy spent a fortune searching for me, he brought me here. I didn't ask to be invited, and I came because he seemed an old man and it wouldn't do any harm to let him have what he wanted for the last few years of his life."

" *Or* to inherit whatever share you thought that such considerateness would earn," suggested Mannering.

Merrow clenched his fists, and Mannering was ready to dodge away from a blow, but none came. Merrow said between his clenched teeth :

" All right, and why not ? Repeat : I didn't look for Uncle Jimmy, he looked for me. I didn't know that he existed as my uncle. I expected to get along under my own steam. Then I came here for what I knew might be six months or six years or longer, and anything I got for burying myself in this god-forsaken part of the world, I'd earned. Yes. I like money. Are you just a philanthropist yourself?"

Mannering chuckled.

"The merit of true honesty," he observed. "There is little that I like better. You expected to be shot at and in danger, didn't you?"

Merrow didn't answer.

"The difficult thing to believe is that there were two distinct motives for the attacks—one for that on you, one for that on Mr. Garfield," Mannering said flatly. "Mr. Merrow, you hardly know me and have no reason at all to take my word, but I shall not lie to you." He paused; then added with a kind of dignity: "I am acting now as an agent of Hodderburn, White and Hodderburn who would of course, as solicitors, respect any confidence you placed in them. There is no need for me to tell the police anything that you voluntarily tell me, or in fact, that I discover. Yet if you were to explain the motive for the attacks on you and I were to tell the police that I was fully satisfied, it would ease the pressure which they will almost certainly exert."

Merrow still didn't answer.

Silence dragged on.

"I hope to come and see you again tomorrow," said Mannering, at last, and stood up. "Now I must go and look after Miss Woburn. She shows very little outward sign of the great strain, does she?"

He stood up.

"What strain?" Merrow demanded sharply.

"We-ell," said Mannering, pursing his lips when he finished, and looking down at the injured man with a kind of fatherly concern, "I'm not sure that the doctors or the police would approve of this confidence, but——" He shrugged. "Miss Woburn has already proved her steady nerve and her great personal courage, but there comes a stage when courage breaks. I wish she looked more nervous, or at least showed her nervousness more; then if she did crack it would be much less harmful."

Merrow said thinly : " She freed my leg. She found Gedde dead and my uncle hurt. What else has she got to fear ? "

Mannering put the tips of his fingers together ; the skin at the backs of his hands was slightly wrinkled, from a drying lotion, so that they did not look the hands of a young man.

He was deliberately long-winded.

" After all, she has no personal relationship with anyone here, and she hasn't worked for your uncle long enough to have a sense of family loyalty. The—ah—unhappy fact is that she saw one or two men who attempted to kill her, surely you knew that. So did a man named Mannering. I believe the newspapers said that it was a road smash, but it went rather deeper. As a result of it, presumably because she can identify these men for the police, she has been put in a position of great danger. So has Mannering. In fact Mannering's wife has been severely injured, and he was hurt in a bomb explosion. Such ruthlessness ! It is difficult to assess the extent of the danger to Miss Woburn, of course, but she has a police guard day and night, and is followed by the police wherever she goes. There was one outside the window when she was here just now."

Mannering paused again.

Merrow was quite still ; hating all this.

" That is why we are all so anxious to find out who is attacking her," Mannering finished quietly. ": At the moment, the police have to spend a lot of time and manpower on checking your past. If you told the simple truth that manpower might be released for the other task, of finding the men who would like to see Miss Woburn dead. Perhaps when I see you tomorrow, you will have decided——"

He broke off, and went to the door.

When he began to open it, Merrow called roughly : " Wait a minute. Come here."

Mannering hesitated.

He judged from the tone of the sick man's voice that

he wasn't in a mood to argue any more. Part of Merrow's trouble came from the bad time he'd had with his leg, but there must have been a lot on his mind before that, and possibly a great deal on his conscience; as on his uncle's. The important thing now was to persuade him to tell everything he knew, to handle the situation so that he would not switch off, abruptly, in a defiant refusal to talk. Obviously, he was a creature of mood; it would take very little to sway him one way or the other.

Mannering turned, and began to say:

" I haven't known Miss Woburn for long, I admit, but if we can't find a way to help her——"

He hoped that would do the trick.

It might have done, but for the interruption.

He heard footsteps, muffled by the hard rubber flooring of the passage, but didn't look round. He assumed it was a nurse. The door had a hydraulic hinge, and he let it swing behind him, intent only on his effect on Merrow.

The door didn't close.

He smelt a whiff of perfume, heard a rustle of movement followed by a startled:

" Oh, I *am* sorry! I didn't know anyone was with you."

Mannering saw Merrow staring at the girl, his expression blank at first, then twisting in a wry grin. Mannering glanced down at her. She had fair hair and bright, shiny make-up and a bountiful figure.

This was the maid, Priscilla, and girls didn't come any prettier or more provocative.

" I could come back——"

" You come right here, Prissy," ordered Merrow, " and hold my hand. Tight. You may have saved me from making a grave mistake, this Mr. Richardson has a persuasive tongue." His smile was still twisted wryly as he looked at Mannering. " If I think I can help any way at all, I'll send a message."

That was final; and there was nothing Mannering could do to change it.

Priscilla looked at him pleadingly, as if knowing she had upset him, but unwittingly—and as if she were trying to apologise. He shrugged and went out. He remembered the note of passion underlying the scene between Merrow and Joanna Woburn. A woman would say that you could never tell with a man. He wasn't so sure. Merrow wasn't acting in character over the maid ; there had been defiance in his manner, a defensive attitude which suggested that he had been badly hurt and could only think of hurting back.

But was that the explanation ?

Mannering wondered if Joanna had seen the girl come along, and if she had, what she would feel.

He reached a corner.

One look at Joanna's set face told him that she had seen Priscilla go into the ward, and didn't like it.

The detective escort appeared to be completely oblivious.

15

THE QUIET OF THE NIGHT

MANNERING PUT DOWN THE RECEIVER OF THE EXTENSION telephone in his room, and sat back in a comfortable chair. He was fully dressed, but his shoes were off; a pair of his own slippers were in the fender, but he hadn't put them on. He was smiling, for the Night Sister at the hospital in Chelsea had been wholly reassuring. Lorna was sleeping naturally, and the signs were good; not a definite all-clear yet, but very promising.

He brooded over that walk along the Embankment.

His mood hardened.

He went over all that had happened during the day, and wasn't sure that he yet had everything in the right perspective. Merrow was one puzzle, Joanna another. Undoubtedly a curious bond existed between them, as if intense dislike and deep affection lived side by side.

Joanna had said little when they had returned to the house. Nothing had happened on the road. They'd dined together in the big dining-room, partly at Mrs. Baddelow's insistence; then Joanna had excused herself, pleading a headache, and gone to her room.

That was next door to Mannering's.

Adjoining on the other side of Joanna was a room with a communicating door, and one of the Orme policemen would spend the night in there. Another was on duty outside, making a regular patrol of the grounds.

Were these precautions enough?

A clock struck ten as Mannering pushed his feet into his slippers, and went outside. No one was in sight. He tried the handle of Joanna's door; she had locked it, as the police requested. So no one could easily get in that way; one detective was at hand, the other outside.

Mannering went downstairs, still uneasy in spite of the precautions. The danger for himself had eased, but he could see that of the girl's more vividly. It was bad enough to know that she might be attacked; to think of her dead . . .

He went downstairs, and found White, the policeman-butler, coming out of the dining-room.

"Everything set, White?"

"I think so, sir."

"The place is thoroughly wired for burglar alarm, I suppose?"

"Oh, yes, thoroughly, sir."

"No weaknesses that you've discovered?"

"We had a Landon man over here this morning, checking and servicing the whole system, and we had double sensitivity arranged for Miss Woburn's room—door *and* window. If anyone gets at her——" White shrugged. "They won't, sir."

"How about the grounds?"

"One man there now, sir, and a second to come at midnight, when we've bedded down." White managed to convey the impression that he thought 'Mr. Richardson' was being excessively fussy.

"It seems fine," Mannering said, "but still——"

"You *really* needn't worry, sir."

Mannering said mildly: "I hope you're right, you know. We can't check and double check enough." His pause puzzled White, and then he added very softly: "She's too young to die."

White caught his breath.

"I don't mean to say that I don't fully understand the importance of it, sir."

"That's good," said Mannering. "Now, what about the roof?"

"That's easy, sir. Mr. Garfield kept the top floor empty and there are only three staircases down. We've sealed each off, sir—no possible danger at all."

What *could* go wrong?

"It all sounds impregnable," Mannering conceded. "I

know I'm an old fusspot, but what about the staff? I gather they've all been thoroughly checked."

"Mr. Aylmer did that himself, sir, and one of the gardeners was stood off yesterday morning—nothing known against him, but he isn't known around here, and the Super was playing safe. Miss Woburn authorised it, sir. All the other people are local, known them all our lives, so to speak—'cept Mrs. Baddelow, and she's been checked. And they're pretty angry. Mr. Garfield is very popular, and all of them have got very fond of Miss Woburn. Everyone's on the alert."

"What time will you lock up?"

"Midnight sharp," answered White. "We're waiting for old Jake, the odd job man, and Prissy—Priscilla. Usually get back on the eleven o'clock bus, I'm told, so they should be here at any minute." He was beginning to sound impatient again. "Might as well go and have a look."

"If you don't mind," said Mannering apologetically, "I'll come with you."

They went out of the front door, and walked round to the side; it seemed a long way. Suddenly, a small light appeared, swaying up and down; soon it was apparent that someone was walking up a secondary drive, swinging a torch. The light seemed to get brighter and whiter. Soon, they could see the outline of two people, a man and a woman. Mannering left White, went inside, and contrived to be at the back entrance when the couple came in.

Jake was elderly and reliable.

Priscilla was flushed, as if she had had a drink or two, and her eyes were very bright. Like that, she looked more than provocatively attractive; she was positively seductive. She was small and virile and vivacious, and it was easy to imagine a man finding solace in her arms.

Solace for *what*?

Mannering gave the girl time to get to her room, after having a cup of cocoa in the kitchen, then asked Mrs. Baddelow to take him up to the staff bedrooms. Mrs.

Baddelow was primness and propriety itself, but didn't object too much when Mannering said that he wanted to talk to Priscilla on her own.

Mrs. Baddelow opened the door, keeping Mannering outside.

" You're not undressing yet, Prissy, are you ? "

" Just going to start. Can't I go to bed when I like, or——"

" Now I don't want any sauce from you," Mrs. Baddelow said sharply. " Mr. Richardson wants to have a word with you."

" What, that old——" Priscilla broke off, and that was obviously at a sign from Mrs. Baddelow. A giggle, quickly stifled, suggested that Mannering wouldn't get much sense out of her ; but if he were going to get any at all, tonight was the night.

" You can come in," Mrs. Baddelow said ; something in her voice was enough to set Priscilla giggling again.

She was grinning when Mannering went in. Mrs. Baddelow closed the door, but was almost certainly standing just outside it. Listening ? Mannering didn't yet know. He stood looking at the girl, who wasn't at all put out ; two more drinks, and she would be as drunk as could be.

" I don't know what you expect me to tell you," she said. " Coming to something, isn't it, police by day and you by——" She broke off, with a giggle. " See what I mean ? "

" Fond of Mr. Merrow ? " Mannering asked abruptly.

That shook her, and helped to sober her. She hesitated for what seemed a long time, then relaxed ; but she didn't sit down, and she was very wary, with a spiteful look.

" Any of *your* business ? "

" No," admitted Mannering, almost wearily. " Nothing to do with me, Priscilla. I just don't want him hurt any more."

" What do you mean ? "

" He won't tell anyone why he was attacked. If we

don't know—and I mean the police as well as me—we can't help him much if he should be attacked again."

"Why should he be?"

"That's what we're trying to find out."

Priscilla moved slowly towards Mannering. She walked with a slight sway, which must have been impressively undulating from behind. He wasn't sure whether she was putting up an act, or whether her carriage was natural. She had the look of a *gamine*, it was hard to see her as a country girl, the daughter of the keeper of an old hostelry in a village as small as Orme Hill. She put her head on one side. Her lipstick and her eyes glistened. She had touched her eyes slightly with mascara; at one corner, her lipstick was smeared, as it might have been after kissing. She wore a shimmery green dress which was a shade too tight. He knew that she was nineteen, but nineteen could easily mean full maturity.

"Look, mister," she said, "I don't know what you're trying to suggest about Mr. Merrow and me, but I'll tell you something. He's a gentleman, and anything he does is okay by me. You might not think I'm good enough for him, and nor might Miss Woburn, but why should I let that worry me? If I can get him, I'm going to—and I don't mind how I do it. See what I mean?"

She did it so well, with great effrontery; but beneath all that there was ample evidence of nervousness.

The last thing she expected was a laugh.

She got one.

"What's funny?" she snapped.

"Very charming," said Mannering dryly, "and as far as I'm concerned, good luck to you, my dear." He wanted her as an ally, not an adversary. "But that's beside the point. I don't want Mr. Merrow to get hurt any more."

"He won't get hurt while he's in hospital."

"Aren't you guessing a lot?"

She shook her head emphatically.

"*I'm* not guessing," she said. "*George* told me that as soon as I got back you and the police would probably be pestering me with questions; I knew what to expect.

Let me tell you something. *George* didn't say a word to me that would interest you or the police, and if he had, *I* wouldn't say a word. I want him to know that he can trust me, see. Tell that to Miss High and Blooming Mighty Joanna, and see whether he trusts *her*."

Mannering raised his eyebrows; and then chuckled again. That startled her. Taking her completely by surprise, he chucked her under the chin, then patted her cheek.

" Spirited wench, aren't you ? Wouldn't do any man any harm ! But don't make any mistakes about it, Prissy—your George might be in danger, and if you can find a way of helping you'll do more good than harm."

She gulped.

" Why don't you take a walk ? " she asked, and turned away.

Outside, Mrs. Baddelow was looking annoyed because Mannering had kept her there so long. He apologised, humbly, and she went off. He watched her thoughtfully. According to White, Aylmer had checked everyone, and all the staff were local, except Mrs. Baddelow. But they were also approachable, and it was surprising what a supposedly loyal servant would do for money.

He went down to his own room.

He listened at the door of Joanna's room for a few seconds, and heard nothing. He would have liked a word with her, to reassure himself and her, but wasn't sure that it would be wise to disturb her if she were asleep. He closed his own door, and looked out of the window. He could see one of the policemen ; the other, presumably, was on the other side of the house.

The policeman showed up in light from a window.

Beyond the range of the light, it was very dark.

When the lights went out, it was pitch. No one could possibly see the man whom Seale and Greer had sent.

Mannering lay between sleeping and waking. He wasn't sure what the time was, or whether he had slept at all. He felt pleasantly drowsy, perhaps a little too warm. The window was open, and he could see the faint greyness of the sky, but there were no stars; clouds had blown up since the afternoon. Wind came up, suddenly, rustling nearby trees, one gust hit the side of the house quite noisily; and then it died away.

A clock struck.

One—two—three.

He couldn't get off to sleep again. He couldn't be sure that there was no way of breaking into the house, and had a feeling that he had missed an obvious way, perhaps one that he would use in the days of the Baron.

Two men to patrol these grounds weren't enough; if a killer came here, he could wait until both were out of sight and earshot, then get to the window. He would have to spend a lot of time at whatever window he chose, though; and he might set off the alarm. It was one thing to break into a protected house, another to do so when the police both inside and outside were on the alert.

But it could be done.

The *Baron* had done it.

If he wanted to get into this house, knowing what he did of the precautions, what would he do?

He turned over, restlessly, and reminded himself that it wasn't only a question of getting into the house, it was one of getting into Joanna's room.

If he left his own door open, so that he would hear the slightest sound, it might give him more peace of mind. He got up, opened the door a fraction, placed a chair against it so that it couldn't be opened wider without disturbing him, and then went back to bed.

How would he get in?

From the roof, of course, but . . .

A small, nippy man who had worked for Lucien Seale over many years, and who set no limit to the kind of crime he would commit, watched the dark shape of Brook House as Mannering lay restlessly, and all the others were silent. Two or three lights were on, and that

was a nuisance, because he might make a mistake, and
be seen. But when one worked for Seale, one didn't
fall down on the job. There were two reasons; Seale
paid well—much better than most—for success, and
reasonably well for the attempt. He also paid *very*
thoroughly for wilful failure.

Seale could give you away to the police, or could
arrange a little accident which would put you to sleep
and make sure that you didn't wake up any more. There
were all kinds of ways to fix these accidents, and Seale
was a specialist in them all.

The little man, whose name was Brill, watched the
policemen as they moved on their regular rounds, now
and again silhouettes against the lighted windows. It
was so quiet that he could hear their footsteps. There
was never complete silence, it was surprising how far the
sound travelled by night.

He closed in.

He knew that the house was wired for a burglar alarm,
knew the system which had been installed, and was well
aware that he couldn't break through it. But burglar
alarms had their weaknesses, and few people ever worried
about wiring up the *top* windows.

According to his information, they didn't here.

He reached the wall, between two lighted windows,
and the darkness shielded him. He heard footsteps,
coming from each direction, the men would meet not
far away from here, talk for a few minutes, and then go
the rounds again. He had chosen the spot well; there
was a buttress, built to hide a drain-pipe which ran down
from the castellated roof. He climbed it quickly, with
as much ease as a Samoan islander shinning up a tree
for coconuts.

He reached a false window-sill; it served no window
but was there to break the flatness of the wall. Standing
on it, he was level with the first-floor rooms; flat against
the wall, there was no risk of being seen.

He heard the policemen meet and talk. They went on
talking for what seemed a long time. He shifted from

one foot to the other, cursing them silently, until they moved off. He let them get some distance away, and then started to tackle the most difficult part of the climb —up to the roof. The buttress was more slender here, and there were few hand- or footholds.

He climbed up nimbly.

He reached the castellated roof.

He swung himself over, making hardly a sound, and then peered over. He could see the yellow light from the windows. The policemen weren't back yet. He moved away, able to walk quite freely. His company were hatches which could open and lead to the attic floors, and the chimney stacks. He had been carefully briefed, and soon took a diagram of the top of the house from his pocket. Up here, away from the walls, it was safe to shine a torch and to light a cigarette. He did this, just as free from anxiety as he would be in a crowded room.

The wind was very strong up here.

He checked the position on the diagram, then looked for a chimney stack marked with a cross. Like all of them, it was large and square. He moved round, smoking, and checking the position of the stacks, until he found the one which he knew would take him down into Joanna Woburn's room.

He didn't know what the condition would be like.

No open fires were burned in the bedrooms, these days, but that didn't mean that the chimney had been properly swept. Big chimneys like this were never thoroughly cleaned these days; small boys wouldn't go down them with their brushes.

He didn't think of that very deeply.

He finished his cigarette.

He took out a mask, into which was fitted a pair of goggles, and placed it carefully into position. It had no breathing apparatus, but it had a filter, and it would keep dirt, dust and soot out of his eyes, nose and mouth. He adjusted it for comfort, then felt in his pockets for gloves; he put these on, and pulled out a knife.

It was sheathed.

He didn't take it right out, but slid it into his waist-band, through a slot which would hold it securely. Then he flexed his muscles, just as an athlete might before a race.

He moved towards the chimney.

Here, he took the rope, and looped it round the stack, making sure that the knot was secure, and then unwound it, and made another loop. This he slid over his head and one shoulder. It was slack, and quite long enough ; it wouldn't get in his way.

Next he took a piece of chewing-gum from his pocket, stripped off the paper, let it fall. The wind swept it away. He put the gum in his mouth. He was chewing rhythmically by the time he reached the stack, and climbed up. He used his torch, and located the foot and hand holes which had been put there for the chimney boys when the house had been built.

He began to climb down.

Below, Joanna Woburn slept, troubled even in her sleep, with one bare arm outside the bedspread, and outflung, the other hidden. The sheet covered her up to her shoulders. Her hair was loose, for she always uncoiled it at night ; it almost covered the pillow.

She had been a long time getting off.

In a room on one side, was the detective, with the door unlocked.

In the room on the other side was Mannering, with his bedroom door open an inch.

Below, the two policemen met just beneath Joanna's room after each of their patrols.

Outside, there was no sound.

The faint rustle in the chimney did not disturb her.

Brill found it easier to get down than he had expected. The air in the chimney seemed quite clean, and there was good foothold. There were two vents in the walls, which carried some of the smoke to other chimneys, and he did not know that these had been adapted into a ventilation system which was one of the many things that Jimmy Garfield had spent his money on.

It didn't matter, either.

Now and again, he loosened a little plaster, and heard it fall. At first, he heard only the first slight rustle; then nothing. But as he drew nearer the hearth, he heard each tiny piece hit the bottom of the fireplace. For the first time, he began to wonder if he would get away with it.

He knew exactly what he had to do.

Get into the room. *Kill* the girl; there were to be no half-measures, he just had to kill her. If she were asleep, that would be fine. Then he was to climb up the chimney, get to the roof, climb down the way he had come, and get away.

In theory, and when he had planned it, after being given the diagram and assured that the chimney was easy for climbing, he hadn't given it much thought. But now he was closely confined, the sides of the chimney brushed against his shoulders and his hands. Tension grew; with every step he found it more difficult to get a foothold, because of his nervousness.

But he went down.

At last, he trod on the hearth itself.

Now, he had to get down on his knees and then crawl out. He was breathing hard, and that was something he hadn't bargained for; it might disturb the woman.

Nothing disturbed her; she lay sleeping.

He crawled from the hearth, and stood up. He was still chewing.

16

THE RUSTLING

MANNERING HEARD THE WIND STRIKE AGAINST THE WALL and window, and then fade. A long way off there were rustling sounds, but that was all. He lay on his back, eyes closed, willing sleep to come. He had not given up his anxieties, but he could see nothing else that he could do. Entry through the roof was possible, but the top floor had been sealed off; what was there to worry about? He was super-sensitive, partly because of what had happened to Lorna. He saw more clearly what Bristow had been getting at about his mood.

Wise bird, Bristow!

He was almost asleep when he heard another rustling sound, which wasn't quite the same as before. He raised his head, so as to listen more intently. It was very slight, and seemed to come from opposite the foot of the bed, near the chimney.

He sat up.

He heard another slightly different sound, as if something had dropped on the hearth; something so tiny that it made practically no sound at all.

Was it raining?

Ah, that was the sound; rain dislodging plaster which was coming down the chimney. He got out of bed, but could not hear the sound of rain, although the window was open. He went to it; the clouds were there, hiding the stars, but there was no rain.

There it came again.

He went to the fireplace, and was not yet sure that he had cause for worry, there were a dozen possible explanations; an owl in the chimney; the wind, setting up vibration which was sending down tiny chippings of plaster that were already loose. Even the fall of plaster which had been on the verge of falling for some time, but—why was it going on for so long?

It stopped.

He knelt down by the fireplace, and studied the big brass dogs, the swept hearth, the pine logs which made it look as if a fire would be lighted soon. He saw nothing to explain the sounds; no tiny pieces of plaster, no marks of soot, nothing smearing the cleanliness of the hearth.

He frowned as he stood up, feeling worried and uncertain.

He heard a rustling sound again, then stretched out on his stomach and put his head close to the back of the fireplace. He heard rustling and slight creaking.

He scrambled back, making hardly a sound, sprang up and strode to the door. He pulled the chair aside. His breathing was coming so fast that it almost choked him. He pulled open the passage door, and stepped into the lighted passage, the carpet muffling all sound. He stepped past the girl's door, towards the policeman's. He still felt choked. If someone had got in that way, a shout would probably make them slash——

Slash.

He turned the handle of the detective's door, and a new fear crowded in on the others; that the man would wake up with a start, and shout for help.

He wasn't asleep; he was sitting in an easy chair, with a book on his knees, and a revolver in his hand. It covered the door. He looked scared, even behind the gun, and his eyes were huge in a broad face. Mannering put a finger to his·lips, and took a step towards him.

" *Keep back!* " the man whispered.

" Someone in her room," Mannering breathed. " Down the chimney."

The man didn't have to believe him; might even suspect his intentions; if he were trigger happy, it wouldn't help much to have explanations afterwards.

Mannering turned towards the door, and prayed.

He mustn't alarm the man in the girl's room.

5

If there was no man——

He didn't think seriously of that possibility as he turned the handle slowly, acutely conscious of the policeman just behind him, gun at the ready. He opened the door a crack. He saw the faint light, and knew that light would go from this room into the other, and that if a man were in there and looking towards the door——

Mannering opened the door wider.

He looked round, and saw the small man, torch in one hand, the other hand hidden. The man's bent back was towards Mannering. He was close to the bed. His right hand seemed to be raised, as his arm would be if he were going to strike.

"*Turn round!*" Mannering rasped.

It still might be too late——

He saw the tension, the movement, the small body half-turn. He saw the knife, out of its sheath, the torch light glittering on it. He saw the breathing mask. Then the little man swung round, moving the knife, as if at all costs he had to finish his job before he was caught.

The policeman fired.

The knife flashed down, the little man cried out in pain, and staggered away from the bed. Mannering rushed towards the bed, seeing Joanna Woburn as the little man moved.

She woke up.

Mannering, still 'Mr. Richardson' to the life, watched as the little man stood in the room next door, with White questioning him, the other policeman standing by. The bullet had caught the man in the shoulders, and they had given him first aid; but the white bandage was already showing signs of crimson.

The prisoner didn't say a word.

With his mask off, he was just a pale-faced, plain little creature, with dark eyes and a nervous manner, thin lips, and the rather raw look that some killers had. His hands and knees were scratched, where he had come down the chimney.

He hadn't said anything that mattered, just insisted on seeing a doctor and a lawyer. He wasn't truculent, in fact he was scared ; but he was adamant, and none of White's cajolery or loud-voiced threats or reasoning had the slightest effect on him.

" What about a doctor, my shoulder's hurting."

" I hope it hurts a damned sight more. Who sent you ? "

Silence.

" Look here, it won't do you any good in the long run, and if you help us all you can now, it'll go easier for you," White said. " Where did you get that diagram of the roof ? "

" It was given to me."

" Who by ? "

" Listen," the little man said, " where's that doctor, I'm losing an awful lot of blood."

Mannering went out of the room. He heard a low-pitched voice in the next room, which was Joanna's, and the door was ajar. He tapped, and when Mrs. Baddelow said " Come in " he opened it wider. Mrs. Baddelow, in a dressing-gown and with her grey hair mousy and untidy without its bun, was sitting in an easy chair by the side of Joanna's bed ; there was a tray with two glasses of hot milk in metal holders on it. Joanna picked up a glass.

" Feeling more yourself ? " Mannering asked.

" The things Miss Woburn's had to put up with while she's been in this house is something awful," Mrs. Baddelow said. Her voice was strident, as if she resented being gazed upon by a male in such a state of untidiness. " The police actually let a *man* get into her room ! If I had my way I'd tell them a thing or two. I think she's *marvellous*," Mrs. Baddelow went on, and glowered as if she expected the remark to be challenged. " The way she stands up to all *this*."

Mannering said : " You're not alone in thinking she's marvellous. How are you, Miss Woburn ? " He went to her.

She said in a low-pitched voice : " More frightened than I ever thought I could be. If they can get in here——"

" It was obvious, really, down the chimney," Mannering said. " The problem "—he looked at Mrs. Baddelow thoughtfully—" is how he knew what chimney to choose. Had them swept lately, Mrs. Baddelow ? "

" No, not since I've been here, except the ones in the library and the dining-room."

" Who sweeps them ? "

" A man from Orme. All electric, but don't you believe it when he says there's no soot, the place was *smothered* ! And I don't mind telling you that he's been sweeping chimneys in Orme for twenty years to my knowledge ; I don't know what you're getting at."

Mannering said : " Just trying to help." He went out, convinced that it was pointless to say anything else to Joanna Woburn. There was just one good thing that might come out of this : Merrow might be persuaded to talk. A visit to Merrow was on the agenda for first thing in the morning.

He looked at his watch. It was nearly six, and he hadn't slept for more than three hours, if as much. The police were handling the prisoner, and even if he had any constructive ideas, they probably wouldn't be welcome. He went back to his own room. The wind was much louder, and he could hear it sweeping across the parkland, howling now and again on a high note which was almost frightening.

If the wind had been up like this an hour or so ago, he wouldn't have heard that rustling.

It was getting near daylight ; the pitch darkness had gone, and he could just make out the shape of trees and the pale outline of the gravel drive. He heard the policeman talking, down below.

He went back to bed.

It was impossible to be sure what would happen next ; impossible to be sure that any precautions were good enough. The unknown man was going to kill at all costs.

And he was going to use men who were ready to take the risk, and wouldn't talk when they were caught.

This one might crack——

Mannering knew that it wasn't likely. You could pick out men who were likely to break down under pressure, and those who would hold out.

He stretched himself out in bed luxuriously. At least there was nothing more to worry about tonight.

He willed sleep ; and now, it came.

Seale knotted his brown tie in front of the dressing-table mirror of his Hampstead house, tugged it too tightly, and then looked out of the window. It was nearly ten o'clock. The rush of traffic into London had really started. A string of buses went noisily, splashing and shimmering in the heavy rain. A cyclist in oilskins pedalled on, obviously unable to see more than a few yards ahead of him because of the big sou'wester.

Seale went downstairs.

His face was set and looked more unreal than ever; shiny, too, where he had washed. His eyes were dull. He reached the foot of the stairs and turned slowly and with deliberation which a robot might have used. He heard the yellow-haired woman, Nancy, talking to some-one out of sight. That was in the kitchen. The telephone was in a room which faced the stairs.

He moved towards the kitchen.

The telephone bell rang.

He turned round, and it was almost painful to see his movements—it would have been easy to believe that each one hurt. He clenched his teeth and parted his lips as he stared at the door of the room where the telephone was. Then he moved towards it, but before he was inside Paul Greer came hurrying from the kitchen, in a puce coloured shirt and cream tie and flannels with a beautiful sharp crease.

" You going to take it ? " he asked.

" No. You."

" Okay." Greer pushed past the big man. The

telephone was on a table just behind the door. Seale watched as Greer lifted the receiver, and said : " Hallo ? "

He paused.

He flashed a glance at Seale, and told him that it was a call that mattered. Both men seemed to go stiff ; and sweat broke out on Greer's forehead.

He said thinly : " *What ?* "

There was a long pause, but his expression told Seale what there was to know. Seale clenched his hands so tightly that his nails hurt his palms ; and the veins in his neck stood out like whipcord. His breathing came hissingly through his broad nostrils.

" You sure ? " Greer asked.

There was another pause.

" Okay," he said. " Nothing—no, nothing yet. I'll call you." He put the receiver down slowly. Then he rubbed his hands together ; they were sticky. He stared into Seale's eyes, and he was afraid.

" He missed her," he said thinly.

" Where is he ? "

" On a charge."

" On a—*charge* ? "

" That's right. They caught him. He did everything, got into the room, was just going to kill her, and they caught him. It was the police and the Richardson guy. They caught him." Greer kept repeating that as if he couldn't really believe it. " He's on a charge, at Orme Police Station. Aylmer's sent for the Yard, dunno who's going there, but someone is."

Seale didn't speak.

" There's one thing," Greer said, with a grotesque effort, " Brill won't talk. He's good that way, he won't talk." His expression changed, it was as if he had said something which he knew might please Seale. " None of the boys will talk."

Seale began to move again ; creakily.

" Mannering ? "

" No news of Mannering," Greer said. " He's just vanished. We've got a couple of men working all the nursing-homes, but that'll take a hell of a time, you can't go in and ask. We're doing the West End ones first. The thing about Mannering is, he——"

Greer stopped.

"Let's have it," Seale demanded.

Greer moved, and eased his neck. The news had come as a severe shock, had affected him as badly as it had Seale, but he seemed to have recovered more quickly.

"Mannering might be dead," he said.

"When I know someone who's seen Mannering buried, I'll believe he's dead," Seale told him gratingly. "Dead, nothing. Lying low. Is he a fool?"

"We can't do a thing if we don't know where he is."

"We don't seem to be able to do a thing if we know where anyone is," Seale said. "That girl's moved about, hasn't she? She's been up and downstairs, she's eaten, she's had a bath, maybe she's taken a walk, maybe she's been out for a drive."

"She saw Merrow yesterday."

Seale moistened his lips. "She gets herself a nice time, and the men I pay good money to watch her move around. Maybe they like her figure."

"Listen, Lucien, it was all laid on——"

"It wasn't done," Seale said. "It's got to be done. What do we have a stooge down there for if it isn't to take risks? Come on, tell me."

"We can't take too many chances. We haven't all that number of men."

"We can take chances," Seale said. "We've got to finish them both. Find Mannering, find the girl, finish ——" He paused, and then went on very softly: "Do you think I'm doing this for fun?"

"Don't be a fool, Lucien. You want to take it easy, you want a rest——"

"Paul," Seale said, "that woman's down there, at Orme. We can make sure that she never leaves Orme. We'll have to sacrifice an agent. Okay, that's what we'll do. Get rid of her. Then find Mannering, and——"

"It's not so easy!"

Seale said: "It's got to be done."

17

Mannering stood at the front entrance of Brook House, looking over the parkland and the drive. The wind was still high, but the clouds had gone and the sun had the brightness which follows rain. The grass was vivid, and seemed very close ; and the trees reflected the hard brightness of the sun. A motor-mower was working out of sight ; there was no other sound near by, but not far off, over a lawn, one of Aylmer's policemen walked, in a frustrated searching for some unknown, even unsuspected clue.

Mannering moved to the top of the steps.

He was thinking of the girl, still in her room. No one could be surprised that she was in a state of prostration. The doctor, elderly and white-haired and rather fussy, had ordered complete quiet and rest. Aylmer, so shaken by Brill's way of forcing entry, had a man at her door, another at her window, another at the door of the adjoining room ; and two men all the time in the grounds. No one quite could guess which way an attack might come next time.

Aylmer had just gone back to Orme ; harassed, nearly bad tempered. He had asked the Yard for help, and no one had yet arrived. He was probably taking a beating from his Chief Constable and he would certainly take one from the Press. If you hadn't been directly involved in the night's raid, it seemed fantastic that the police couldn't have kept one man out.

The thing that most worried Mannering was the diagram. It had been drawn fairly recently, because the paper was fresh and white ; but it might be a copy of an older drawing. Its accuracy was remarkable. It could only have been sketched by someone who had been up on the roof, or had copied a photograph or plan of it. No one remotely associated with Brook House, in Orme, could recall a plan of the roof having been prepared. The chimneys were swept each year, but only four were used regularly ; and the bedroom chimneys hadn't been cleaned for years ; they were used mostly for ventilation.

So, who had been up there ?

One of the staff ? That was an obvious possibility. Mrs. Baddelow ? Mannering let her name drift in and out of his mind. He had talked to Aylmer about the housekeeper, and been assured that she came from a nearby town, was very well known, had a thoroughly good reputation. Merrow ? Well, Merrow might have been up to the roof, but had anyone known of the need for the diagram before Merrow's injury ? That was a question Mannering couldn't answer, but one thing gradually made itself clear. If anyone had wanted to break into Brook House for an ordinary burglary, the one possible way was from the roof—and the one way in which it would be almost impossible to raise an alarm was through a chimney. By night, the supposed impregnable house was in fact easily entered. Most ' impregnable ' houses were to men with daring and skill.

When had the diagram been drawn ? And by whom ? If Merrow, how had it come into Brill's possession ? If Merrow, why had Merrow been attacked ?

Mannering stopped guessing, and went down to the drive, then walked towards the garages at the back. He didn't hurry. The sun was warm. He saw a small van outside the garage, with a picture of a grey horse on either side, and when he drew nearer, he saw the words ' Grey Mare '. A man whom he had seen casually once or twice was lifting a small barrel of beer from the back of the van. Seated inside the van, ears cocked, eyes fixed on Mannering, was the big Alsatian.

" Afternoon, sir," the man greeted.

"Good afternoon." Mannering smiled as Mr. Richardson might be expected to smile, and went to the antiquated

Austin. He remembered being told that the big man was Jeff Liddicombe, Priscilla's father. That had him thinking about Priscilla, showing her claws. When one looked at her casually, it didn't seem possible that she had such strength of purpose ; the feline had shown almost savagely when she had talked to him.

Who had drawn that diagram ?

Could a tradesman get access to the roof ? Had any building been on the roof lately ? When had there last been decorating work done ?

He drove off, slowly, down the drive, quickening his pace when he reached the road. Orme was nearly half an hour away, because of a winding road. The inn sign of the ' Grey Mare ' was swinging in the wind and the gravel outside it seemed deeper yellow because of the rain.

He drove straight to the hospital. No one bade him nay, and he went to Merrow's ward. Outside some wards was a card, reading ' Engaged ' ; no card hung on the handle of Merrow's door.

Mannering went in.

Merrow was reading a newspaper.

He looked up, recognised ' Mr. Richardson ', but didn't put the paper down until Mannering was half-way across the room. He had been shaved, and looked much more presentable than he had the previous afternoon.

" What do you want ? " he asked gruffly.

Mannering didn't pull a chair, but stood at the foot of the bed. His confidence in his disguise was complete now ; no one here had looked twice at him, he was absolutely sure that they did not dream that he was anything but the middle-aged man he looked.

He said : " A man named Brill climbed down Miss Woburn's chimney last night, and——"

Merrow dropped the newspaper. " *No !* " His eyes showed all the terror any man could feel.

" . . . and attempted to kill her. More by luck than judgment, she was saved." Mannering kept his voice very flat. " She's now in a state of collapse, and likely to stay that way if we can't take this load off her mind soon. She can't keep it back any longer, she's afraid of being killed. She knows that someone is going to stop at nothing to kill her. So do I."

Mannering stopped. Merrow hadn't attempted to look away from him.

Mannering let the silence drag out, wanting Merrow to speak next. He judged the inward battle that the man was fighting, wondered what caused his obstinacy and his defiance.

Then Merrow said: "I don't know that I can help at all."

"You could try."

"That's right," Merrow said, "I could try, and perhaps do more harm than good. I don't know. What I've told you is true. I am Garfield's nephew. I have travelled a great deal. I have also spent four out of the past five years in a South African jail."

He flung those words out.

Mannering said: "A lot of men have been in jail without becoming misanthropes. What did you get jailed for?"

"Making a fool of myself."

"They gave you a stiff sentence for that," Mannering murmured.

Merrow said: "I trusted a woman. I was looking around for a new gold stake in the Transvaal. I thought I'd make one. I played safe, as I thought, and got my girl friend to influence some capital for it. I hadn't enough. If I'd known Jimmy Garfield then, I could have asked him, but I didn't know I had a millionaire uncle. I put all I'd got into this—nearly three thousand pounds. I had a prospectus drawn up, and, under cover of secrecy, got a lot of investment capital subscribed. My girl and her friends banked it for me, they said.

"Then I published the details of the field. But there wasn't any gold. I'd been played for a sucker. The little beauty had robbed me of everything, including my good name. She even squeezed herself out of it, she put

up such an act in court—*I* was the double-dyed villain.
She was as beautiful as Delilah, and twice as——"

He broke off.

Mannering said very gently : " And you served your
sentence for fraud."

" That's right. I was in jail when Uncle Jimmy's men
caught up with me."

" Does he know about the prison sentence ? "

" He does."

" So he's broadminded."

" We talked about it only once," Merrow said slowly,
" and he's never referred to it again. All he said was
that he'd done some things in his life he was ashamed of.
He'd once cheated a young man out of a few thousand
pounds, and the youth committed suicide. He had a row
with another man over it—his accomplice. He——"

" Did he name the youth he'd swindled ? "

" No."

" The accomplice ? "

" No."

" Did he say anything more about it ? "

" It was nearly twenty years ago, and the accomplice
was sentenced to three years' imprisonment," Merrow
said flatly. " He said he'd tried to make amends but
been rebuffed." For a moment, Merrow hesitated, and
there was a searching, longing look in his eyes. " No,"
he added at last, " he didn't mention any name."

Mannering decided not to press the question.

" What about these attacks on you ? " he asked.

Merrow said : " They were to scare the wits out of
me."

" Why ? "

" Some of the crowd I was mixed up with before discovered who I was, and came back to England. They
suggested that I should let them into the house one night,
so that they could make off with everything they could
lay their hands on. It was all nice and specious. I
needn't be involved. Uncle Jimmy would be insured,
so no one but insurance companies would suffer, and who

cared about them? They said that if I did it, I'd get a quarter share. If I didn't, they said they'd got something on Jimmy that would send him to jail for the rest of his life."

Mannering said sharply:

" Had they ? "

Merrow answered:

" The truth is, I don't know. I couldn't risk going to the police, the old boy had been so decent."

" What did you say to these people ? "

Merrow said savagely : " I told them to go to hell, I wouldn't play. They tried to scare me. Threats, shots which just missed, car accidents which weren't really serious but could have been. I could have told the old man, but it wasn't only the threat they made. His heart isn't good, and—well, I thought if I held out, they'd get tired of it. They weren't likely to kill me while they still hoped I'd play—wasn't that reasonable enough ? "

" Very," Mannering agreed.

" I kept toying with the idea of telling the police, but put it off," said Merrow. " I'd no reason to believe that anyone else was in danger."

Mannering said very quietly : " So you just sat back and did nothing at all."

Merrow didn't answer.

" You being you, I don't believe it," Mannering said flatly.

Merrow growled : " You're too clever, aren't you ? One of these days——" He broke off. " All right, I fought back. I knew one thing for certain : it was someone who lived locally. I mean, they used a local man. Someone who knew the district, the copses, the countryside generally. Two or three little things happened that made me think that it might be someone in the house. I suspected them all, from Mrs. Baddelow downwards or upwards, and not excluding Joanna."

He'd suspected *Joanna*.

It came out defiantly, too ; as if Merrow expected to be called a fool ; but what was foolish about it ? Joanna had applied for a job and been accepted, and so she had a wonderful opportunity to spy on Merrow and to do what the unknown men wanted him to do.

" Any proved cause for suspicion ? " asked Mannering.

Merrow snapped : " No. There were times when I hated myself for doubting her. Others when she seemed the obvious suspect. The one certain thing is that some-one in this household spied on and reported my move-ments, and made it damned difficult. I got to the stage of not caring what they did or said, just hoping that it would come to an end. When I caught my leg in that trap——"

Mannering said : " Could Joanna Woburn have put the traps down ? "

" No ! "

" Could she ? "

" *I said no !* "

" I was hoping for an honest answer," Mannering said.

Merrow growled at him : " Damn you, why have a down on her ? Supposing she could ? She didn't. Aylmer's told me that those traps were in the Museum Bar at the ' Grey Mare ' at lunchtime on the day they were used. Joanna couldn't have gone there, collected them, and set them."

" They could have been collected and put somewhere convenient for her."

" Well, I don't believe she had anything to do with it," Merrow said, " and yet——" His mouth twisted ; for a moment he looked positively ugly. " Well, how the hell can I be sure ? One woman who looked as whole-some as she does was bad right through. Joanna could be, too."

" Could have been," Mannering corrected.

" I don't understand you."

" Doubts about Joanna can be put out of your mind," Mannering reassured him. " She's been attacked twice, and last night was touch and go. If she worked for these men, they wouldn't attack her this way, would they? I don't think there's a lot of reason to doubt Joanna, you can forget that one."

Merrow closed his eyes. The newspaper rustled, and then slid off the bed to the floor. Merrow lay on his back, his lips set tightly. He was a man to pity; and he looked both strong and helpless as he lay there.

18

DISCOVERIES BY BRISTOW

BRISTOW SWUNG ALONG THE PASSAGE AT NEW SCOTLAND Yard towards the Assistant Commissioner's office, and those who knew him well knew also that Bristow had his tail up. The Assistant Commissioner, a leathery-looking military man fairly new to his post, who was beginning to know him well, motioned to a chair, and greeted:

"What's the excitement about?"

"I think we're getting somewhere on the Garfield job," Bristow said.

"Thanks to the genius of your friend Mannering?"

"Partly," said Bristow, and allowed himself a slightly caustic reproof. "If we had a dozen men as good as Mannering here, we'd be in clover. He's been digging deep and he's got Merrow to talk. Here's the story——"

The Assistant Commissioner, a meticulous man, made notes in a neat hand. They read:

G. Merrow convicted of fraud in South Africa, blames associates, says associates now attacking him.

Prisoner caught at Brook House named Brill, twice convicted of crimes of violence. Killer.

Bristow was still talking:

"I've cabled Johannesburg, and should get a reply today, for information about the gold-field fraud. That'll give us the names and known movements of the people concerned in that job."

"Good," approved the Assistant Commissioner solemnly.

"Then we've got Brill," said Bristow. He said that with mingled satisfaction and reserve. "Brill won't talk and nothing will make him. It's hardly worth while trying. I've been through his record, and he's never made a helpful statement when on a charge. Before he went down on the last job for seven years—he got his remission and came out two years ago—he was on a charge of attempted murder. By opening his mouth, he could have saved himself. He didn't; he kept loyal. Never sure whether it is loyalty or because they just hate our guts," Bristow said with feeling, " but we come across a lot of Brills, and this time we seem to have struck something really ugly."

He waited for a reaction.

" Go on, please," said the Assistant Commissioner formally.

" The man who fell down the stairs at Mannering's place and broke his neck also had a bad record," Bristow told him. " His name was Byall. He'd been inside for robbery with violence. He was another silent type. Both of these men were as vicious as they come. They were killers. They took chances that would have scared ninety-nine men in a hundred. They weren't up against it for money—both of them ran bank accounts and had several hundreds of pounds to their credit, and they got regular payments. Brill didn't say anything to us, but at the banks they were supposed to make their living by betting. More likely, they were on a pay roll." Bristow was so intent on what he was saying that he lit a cigarette without waiting for approval; and the A.C., who missed nothing, let it pass. The Superintendent's excitement was infectious. " Now and again some of us get together and try to sort out the kind of stuff we're likely to come up against," Bristow went on. " Did so only a few weeks ago, when we picked up Benny Duvanto for the King Street killing. Benny was another of this type. There aren't twenty of them in the country, as far as we know—and they're more explosive and more dangerous than two thousand ordinary crooks."

The A.C. said sharply: " Exaggerating, Bristow ? "

" Considered opinion," Bristow nearly snapped.

" You mean, we *do* have hired killers who have neither compunction nor fear ? "

" That's about it," Bristow agreed.   " We know where most of them are, and keep them under survey as far as we can ; but we can't keep them in the country or tabs on each one.   Now we know that two were in this job, and we also know that they knew one another. It could be that several others, still free, are mixed up in this job, and if they are——"

He didn't finish.

" What are you going to do ? " asked the Assistant Commissioner.

" Have each one we know checked and followed," Bristow said.   " Can't do more, sir.   With the bit of luck we need, we'll have some names to play with to-night.   No need to worry you with the rest of the story —except that I've been talking to Mannering on the telephone, and he takes the same view as me."

" What's that ? "

" That the two men he and Miss Woburn saw when she was held up on the road made a big mistake in letting themselves be seen, that it wouldn't matter unless they wanted to appear pretty freely in public.   So Mannering thinks they're likely to be involved in a big fraud, and that the box of so-called miniatures taken from Garfield is a key to it."

" Hm, yes, could be," conceded the Assistant Commissioner.   " Garfield been able to talk yet ? "

" The doctors say that he can't be questioned for another four or five days.   He's come round twice, each time almost lucid, but he's still on the danger list.   Any ordinary man would have been dead by now."   Bristow stubbed out his cigarette and, without thinking, lit another.   " I think that covers the essentials, sir."

" Good.   Any news of that small car which Miss Woburn fired at ? "

" No."

" No other local developments ? "

" I'm in touch with Aylmer regularly, and we've sent Marble down there to help out," said Bristow.   " I don't think Aylmer will miss much.   He has photographs where we have them and general descriptions of the bad men we have on our list, and if he recognises anyone, he'll be on to us like a shot. The trouble with most of the photographs is that they're old."

"We don't seem to be missing many angles," the Assistant Commissioner conceded.

Bristow went back to his own office, not dissatisfied. His desk was cleared of everything except papers relating to the Garfield job; there was a limit to the amount that one man could do. He had seldom felt more edgy. One met ruthlessness of the kind being shown in this job one, two or three times in a lifetime; and when faced with it, the outlook was bad.

All the precautions in the world couldn't be guaranteed to save Joanna Woburn or Mannering, once Mannering was known. Bristow knew it. Unless the men were caught in time, more murder was inevitable.

Bristow's chief worry was not knowing how much time he had to work in.

If he could get one break, such as find the car with the bullet mark in the back, for instance, it might make a world of difference.

He telephoned the hospital in Chelsea, received a good report on Mannering's wife, and replaced the receiver.

As he did that, a constable in the greater London area was examining the back of a small car which had a peculiar mark in the back. He only noticed it because at the station that morning they'd been briefed to look for small, dark cars with a bullet mark or indentation on the back. Turning a corner near Hampstead Heath, he had seen a car parked outside a house at an angle which showed the mark.

The constable was P.C. Wilberforce, attached to the Hampstead Police Station, a middle-aged, unambitious officer who knew his job from A to Z and had no desire to get stripes and have to learn a new alphabet. The fact that some years before he had inherited what was, for him, a comfortable little sum so that he and his wife and three children could live in comparative comfort, was an important influence.

Wilberforce had a conscience and did his job thoroughly, but made no attempt to step outside his own limits.

The car was an elderly Hillman 10. It was parked outside one of the older houses near the Heath, on a slight rise ; that, and the slanting morning sun, had shown up the mark. No one else was about, although the rattle of milk bottles sounded near by ; probably the milkman and his float was in the drive of a house, or round a corner. The house was three doors away from crossroads.

Wilberforce, a thin man who looked too small for his uniform, hitched up the leg of his trousers, and knelt down to examine the mark more closely.

He knew what bullet marks were like, for before joining the police he had served in the army which had been forced from Dunkirk. He knew the kind of mark that a bullet made on all kinds of metal, too. This one had struck the sheet metal at the back of the car just where it was curving slightly, to vanish beneath the car body. He put his little finger in it. The edge was rather rough. He tried the handle of the boot ; it was just possible that the bullet had stayed inside the boot, *if* this were a bullet hole.

P.C. Wilberforce did not know of any other means by which a hole of that kind could be caused. Just took the tip of his little finger, and that probably meant a ·32 ; the gun used had been a ·32.

Where any other officer would probably have felt excited at the thought that he had made a discovery, Wilberforce experienced just a little mild satisfaction. Lack of ambition, as often, went hand in hand with lack of imagination, and he did not pause to think that he might be in danger.

He did not know that he was being watched.

The first man to see Wilberforce looking at the car was Seale—standing at his favourite place near the window, where he could see the Heath, the passing traffic, and anyone who approached. Seale promptly sent for Greer. Both men watched as P.C. Wilberforce hitched up his trousers and bent down.

"What the hell's he doing?" Seale demanded. "What's at the back of the car?"

Greer began: "Nothing, I shou——" and then broke off abruptly.

"What's the matter, lost your tongue?"

Greer gulped. "I've just thought, there might be——" He was scared by the look in Seale's eyes, but couldn't evade the issue now. "The night I was at Brook House. The woman fired at me, remember. If she hit the back of the car, there would be a mark."

Seale said: "You——" and then shot out a hand and slapped Greer's face. The plump man backed against the wall; the puce of his silk shirt looked deep and bright against the cream-coloured paper.

He didn't speak.

"We've got to get that copper," Seale said, "and we've got to get him fast. You——"

"We can't bring him here!"

Seale said: "Go and get him."

The policeman outside was still on his knees.

Greer said: "We can't bring him here! I don't give a damn what you say, we can't!"

"I tell you——"

"Why the hell don't you let me *think*?"

Seale stopped. Greer looked out of the window, and for a long time they stood quite still. The red mark on Greer's face gradually began to fade.

Then he said: "Freddy's downstairs. We'll have him go and tell the copper that he's found something on the common, will he take a look." Greer paused, as if he were seeking desperately for some weakness in that idea.

The policeman stood up.

"Get it done," growled Seale.

"Okay, okay." Greer turned and hurried downstairs.

He was very light on his feet, but seemed to make a lot of noise that morning.

Seale watched the policeman, who was looking straight at the house and would have seen him but for the net curtain. A milk float passed ; Seale could actually hear the rattle of the bottles.

Then the policeman turned towards the main road, only a hundred yards away. He didn't hurry. His helmet moved along the top of the hedge at an even height and speed. He did not look round.

A minute later, Seale saw a small man pass the gate—a man named Freddy, who had a dossier at Scotland Yard and would have been recognised by Bristow as one of the men on the *Highly Dangerous* list. He was too low for the wall, and was hidden completely, but in a second or two, the helmet stopped, and turned round.

Then it began to move in the opposite direction.

Seale was sweating. . . .

Freddy wasn't sweating. He had a job to do, and he knew exactly what it meant and what the risks were. He felt an excitement which he had strictly under control, but was there. He took a pride in his craft. It did not occur to him that killing a man was really more reprehensible than killing a pig ; he knew the consequences of being caught were much greater, but that was all. He had, in fact, killed at least a dozen times ; had first discovered the excitement and the sadistic satisfaction in it during the war.

Now, it was a battle of wits.

In all respects except his ' craft ', Freddy had a human being's approach to life. The policeman with him was walking unsuspiciously towards the heath because he, Freddy, had told him that he'd found some silver and jewellery in some bushes there ; it looked like a burglar's haul, abandoned during the night. Even an unambitious policeman could feel the urgent need to take notice of that.

Wilberforce, in fact, felt that it was a day when everything would happen at once. He wanted to report that bullet hole in the car, Number 2BN563, and if he turned in news of a burglar's haul too. . . .

They reached the common. Freddy led the way to a clump of bushes. They reached it about the time that Wilberforce realised that no burglary had been reported for several nights, this stuff must have lain here for some time.

Freddy pointed : " You have to bend low to get in— saw something glint, I did, that's what made me curious. I shall get a reward, shan't I ? "

" If it's worth anything, you'll be looked after," said Wilberforce, and bent low to get through the gap in the bushes. It wasn't low enough, so he went down on his knees. His broad back was a perfect target for the knife ; and Freddy had all the time in the world to select the spot.

Wilberforce just felt something painfully sharp——

19

UNEASY PEACE

MANNERING STUDIED HIS FACE IN THE MIRROR, TWO
mornings after the murder of P.C. Wilberforce, of
which he had read almost casually, and decided that the
stain was wearing off slightly ; he would have to scrutinise
his disguise and touch it up where necessary.

He didn't like the idea.

He had hoped to finish the job here within forty-eight
hours. It was one thing to live the part of another man
for a day or two, another to go on doing it indefinitely.
The strain was greater than he had expected, and was
worse because everyone watched him all the time.

Mrs. Baddelow, after the early hostility, seemed to be
coming round ; she was more amiable, and she had a
habit of slapping his arm and going off into a burst of
laughter at one of his least amusing witticisms ; yet there
was often a sharp glint in her eyes, and he knew that
whatever he did, she noticed ; at least, she tried to.

The police also watched him intently. Here was a
private inquiry agent who, in a way, seemed to be claim-
ing to be able to teach them their job. White had now
developed a mock humility, overdid the ' sir ' and at any
request went off at an exaggerated double. Chief Inspector Hill hardly troubled to conceal the fact that he
thought Mr. Richardson's position to be superfluous. By
far the most amiable of the police was big Superintendent
Aylmer, but he was seldom at the house. The Orme
police were finding the watch on Brook House more of a
strain than they liked ; the total force wasn't large, and
duties which were almost as essential as those here were
being neglected.

Mannering had checked everyone.

He had spent an hour on the past two evenings at the

'Grey Mare'. Mine host was not a particularly hearty type and certainly wasn't servile, but he seemed friendly and genuine. His dog was handsome and aloof. Mannering examined the old barn, now a bar-cum-museum, and some of the relics were interesting even to the casual visitor. A pair of stocks, a gibbet used in far-off days when Orme had been a highwayman's paradise, some old agricultural implements, some bronze coins, a few early Saxon flints, Roman vessels dug up from earthworks between here and Orme, made it genuinely of historical interest. There were a lot of pictures, too, including pictures of the animals which had roamed the district centuries ago. Everything was clearly marked with neat notices in red and white.

The only black spots on the old oak walls were those where the big traps had been hanging.

Mannering went again that midday.

"Don't mind admitting, sir," said Jeff Liddicombe. "It didn't occur to me that anyone would ever want to lift them off the walls. They were secured in anyway, had little chains fixed to 'em—like that old plough over there, and the matchlock beside it—and hung from two nails. Must have nipped in, parked his car right up to the door with the boot open, lifted the traps off—and there you are. Half a minute would be time enough."

"Isn't the barn kept locked?"

"Well, it is and it isn't, if you know what I mean," said Liddicombe. He had a pale, even-coloured face and rather dull eyes—there was just his hair to remind one of Priscilla. "It ought to be kept locked, but we're a bit careless about things like that round here. I've come across it unlocked several times in the past few weeks, and I always tell Ted about it—that's the barman who looks after this bar, sir—but what's the use of dressing him down too much, if *I* forget too, when I'm on duty."

"Fair enough," agreed Mannering. "And the police have worried you enough about it already. I only came for a glass of your excellent beer and to have a look round here. Whose idea was the museum?"

"Well, sir, mine as a matter of fact. I've always had a liking for old things, and when I took over the old 'Grey Mare' two years ago, it gave me my chance. Hardly cost a pound, either. I do all my own lettering, and what stuff wasn't on the premises I've picked up for a song."

"The British Museum should hear of you," Mannering said.

Liddicombe looked pleased.

"That's kind of you, sir. You're welcome to that beer, sir," said Liddicombe. "Mr. Merrow comes most nights when he's at home. Old Mr. Garfield often says he'll come. Proper life of the party, isn't he?" They went together into the main saloon bar, inside the three centuries' old inn. "It's a very bad business, and I can't tell you how sorry I am for that Miss Woburn. Very nice young lady, by all accounts."

"Very."

"Wonderful job she did, opening them steel traps, the springs on them take some forcing if you don't know the trick. And Mr. Merrow wasn't much help, from what I hear, must have been pretty well unconscious. Funny way to end a row." There was a moment's pause, hardly noticeable, before he went on : "And she's had a lot to put up with since. I know what I'd do, if I were in her shoes."

"What ? "

"Get out just as fast as I could," said Liddicombe.

Mannering said : "Ah, yes." He didn't add : "And your daughter Priscilla would like that, wouldn't she ? " In fact, he hardly gave it a thought. He entered the low-ceilinged bar, nodded at the dozen people standing or sitting about, and took the beer in a pewter tankard when Liddicombe offered it to him, and no one could have noticed that he was in any way unusual.

Inwardly, his heart was hammering, his excitement was bottled up.

No one but Aylmer, Merrow, Joanna and he knew about the quarrel before the traps had been sprung.

How did Liddicombe know?

There was a plan of the roof of Brook House beautifully drawn; and Liddicombe was an excellent draughtsman, one who did all the lettering for the exhibits here.

Liddicombe must be checked, urgently.

It was nearly half-past twelve, as dark now as it had been on the night when Brill had come down the chimney. No stars shone, but there was no wind. The police, wearying now in their vigil, were on the move outside. All the ground-floor lights were on, to make it more difficult for anyone to approach without being seen.

It was almost as difficult to leave.

Mannering, wearing an old raincoat turned up at the collar, and a slouch-hat pulled low over his eyes, worked at a window overlooking the garage and the stables; this was the easiest way to leave without being seen. He had disconnected the alarm wires here, and opened the window. From the outside, he hooked the wires together, so that no one looking at them casually would notice that they had been touched. Then he closed the window.

He stood quite still.

His tool kit was round his waist, and he carried a ·32 automatic. He had recovered from the pulsing excitement of early evening, but the heaviness of spirit had eased; he believed that he was on the way.

Patience rewarded. . . .

He heard the policeman on duty on this side of the house walk past; then he slipped out, and for a few seconds was visible in the light from the kitchen windows. He reached the shadows of a beech hedge.

No alarm came.

He walked to the end of the walled vegetable garden, then into the parkland beyond. He had used this path several times, and knew it well; it was the path which Joanna and Merrow had used on the day the traps had been sprung.

The walk to the village took him twenty-five minutes.

He kept on the grass at the side of the road, until he was opposite the old barn near the ' Grey Mare '. No light shone anywhere, but there were rifts in the clouds now, and he could see the stars.

The inn, with its low uneven roof, its outbuildings, its beamed walls, stood squat and solid. The clean gravel and tar yard made it easy to walk with little sound. Mannering went along one side, between the old barn and the main building. He felt cool, yet the excitement still affected him. He reached a spot where he could not be seen from the road if a car passed with its headlights on, and then reached up to a small outhouse, near the back door. In spite of the thick clothes and the big shoes, he climbed up easily, and stood for a moment on the sloping roof, with a gabled window in front of him.

He drew a cotton scarf up over his face, so that only his eyes showed.

The window was closed.

He took out a pencilled torch, with a specially diffused beam, and studied the window ; it was latched, but did not seem to be wired for burglary. He took a slim tool from the kit in his waistband, and inserted it between the two halves of the window, then prised at the catch. It moved slowly. He could hear no other sound, not even from the nearby woodland ; there was just the scraping of metal on metal, and the sound of his own breathing.

The catch moved sharply ; and the window boomed. Mannering stopped working, and listened ; but the seconds brought him relief, and no alarm was raised.

He opened the window.

He shone the torch inside, and found that this was a narrow passage, with bare boards and cream walls ; a staircase head was at one end, a dark door at the other. He put a leg over the window, and climbed through. The danger of night marauding in all old places was always the same ; loose floorboards which creaked ; and in inns particularly they were often left to creak, so as to add to the atmosphere.

A board creaked.

He stepped as close to the wall as he could, and there was no sound. He waited for a few seconds, with a soft wind coming through the window, striking cold on his damp neck. Then he heard a noise a long way off, and gradually it grew louder; the headlamps of a car lit up the road, the telephone wires, the swinging inn sign, the old barn.

The car flashed by.

One could never be sure that one was alone.

Mannering didn't close the window, but stepped towards the head of the stairs. Once or twice boards creaked faintly, but he stopped most of the noise by keeping close to the wall; it slowed him down, but minutes lost now might save disaster.

He actually let that word pass through his mind.

Remember, they were killers.

If he were right, and Liddicombe was involved, Liddicombe was also a killer.

Someone who lived near by, someone who knew what went on at Brook House, someone who could find out what was happening indoors; Liddicombe measured up to all that. He was often at the big house; Priscilla his daughter could tell him what he wanted to know, perhaps without realising why he needed the information.

As Mannering reached the head of the stairs, he reminded himself again—they were *killers*.

He must not make a mistake.

He studied the staircase. It went down only half a dozen steps before reaching a half landing. There were glints from bronze and copper, warming-pans and oddments fastened to the walls; a gem of a place, this 'Grey Mare'.

Where did Liddicombe do his diagrams and his lettering?

There would be an office downstairs, but he probably worked somewhere else.

Find out !

Mannering crept down the stairs. He kept by the

banisters, putting part of his weight on them, and made hardly a sound. Downstairs, it wouldn't be so dangerous. He shone the torch all round, seeing the signs on the doors —Bar, Saloon Bar, Residents' Lounge, Lounge Bar, Reception—Office.

He went to the office.

It was locked.

He took a pick-lock from his pocket, studied the key-hole and then slid the dull steel in. A few twists, and he felt the barrel of the lock going back. He opened the door, very cautiously; it didn't squeak. He stepped inside.

A dog growled deep in its throat and leapt at him.

20

THE DOG AND THE MAN

THE GREEN EYES GLINTED IN THE GLOW FROM
Mannering's torch. He had just that split second of
warning, heard the growl, felt his heart leap wildly—
and then saw the huge, dark shape coming.

Instinctively, he covered his face with his hands.

Teeth tore at his coat.

He felt the cloth rip, felt a painful tear at his right
forearm. By then he was over the worst of the shock,
and knew that if he had a chance he had to make it
now. The dog's first leap was over, it was dropping
back; the deep growl might become a wild bark any
moment.

Mannering shot out his hands, snatching at the thick
neck. The dog snapped, and missed. Mannering's fingers
buried themselves in the fur and the flesh. He felt the
heavy body writhing, the powerful sinews working up
and down. He didn't know whether his thumbs were
at the right spot. He pressed harder and still harder,
keeping the dog at arm's length.

He felt its struggles weaken.

It went limp.

He lowered it, and stood for a moment in the middle
of the office, sweat dripping from his forehead, mouth
wide open as he gasped for breath. He couldn't do a
thing. He knew that he had only seconds in which to
work, but he couldn't start yet.

The dog was quivering.

He hadn't broken its neck and hadn't choked it; it
might come round in seconds; or it might lay there
for minutes. He dropped to his knees, heavily, took a
stretch of cord from his kit, and tied it round the big,
wet muzzle; the cord wasn't tight enough to hurt, but

would stop the dog from biting. He bound the legs together, leaving the cord slack, and then stood up.

He felt better and far less desperate ; no sound came from above, nothing indicated that he had raised an alarm. The dog had been trained to silence ; trained to bring his man down, not to bark.

Mannering looked round, easing his collar.

There was a desk and, in a corner, a small drawing-board with a light immediately above it ; so, this was the right spot.

He wiped his forehead as he stepped to the drawing-board. Pinned to it was a sheet of paper with the outline of a house sketched in, and Mannering recognised it as one end of the ' Grey Mare '. Forget that ! He looked through the paper in a rack, finding dozens of unfinished sketches, some lettering, some tracing paper ; there was no sign of the plan of the top of Brook House. The lettering was not unlike the plan, the ink looked identical, so did the stiff, white drawing paper.

There was nothing else, no way of proving beyond doubt that the plan Aylmer now held had been drawn here ; if he were to give the police evidence, he had to find a copy of the plan.

The safe was in a corner.

He heard the dog moving and grunting.

He went to the door, stepped into the passage, and listened intently ; he heard no sound at all, and felt confident that no one was disturbed ; he still had time. He closed the door of the office ; that would keep the sound the dog made inside. He spoke to it softly, but it only growled ; he could feel it struggling.

He turned to the safe.

It was an old Cobb, and he had opened dozens like it ; but many modern gadgets could make a fool of the expert safe-breaker. He studied it closely ; it looked as easy a crib to crack as he could have hoped for ; child's play for the Baron. He tried his keys, but none was good enough. He found one which seemed to get a little purchase, withdrew it, smeared the surface with a thin tacky white paste from a flat tin, and put it in again carefully.

He turned this as firmly as he could, then let it fall back into its proper position, and withdrew it. Faint marks showed, made by the barrel of the lock against the paste. He put the key in a small steel hand vice, took out a file, and began to work on the key; the noise was negligible.

He had to file three edges.

The lock didn't turn when he tried it again; he touched the key with the file again, and put it back.

It opened.

He saw the bags with the day's takings, the cash boxes, the account books; and none of this mattered; he put all of it aside. He found a large envelope which had no marking on the outside; it wasn't sealed. He took out the contents.

There were two copies of the plan of the roof of Brook House. Several of the chimney stacks were marked, including one serving Joanna's room, one the library; and under that was a note: ' Strong-room through here '. He studied them quickly, and felt quite sure what they implied. Someone had been planning a burglary on a large scale at the house, had studied it closely and decided that the only way in was through the chimneys.

Liddicombe would have a job to get out of this.

Mannering didn't put the envelope back at once, but glanced through other papers with the plans. There were notes about Merrow, Joanna Woburn, Gedde and Garfield; notes about Mrs. Baddelow; the half-days of the servants; the habits and customs of the residents, the staff, all the day's routine. Whoever had studied Brook House had meant to make quite sure that he knew everything.

Only one other document interested Mannering. It was a death certificate of a man named Holden, dated just over ten years ago.

Mannering studied it, shrugged, then put it back, with all the oddments he had taken out of the safe, closed and

6

locked the door. No one would know that it had been open. The next thing to do was to tell Aylmer that it would be worth looking into the safe.

Should he tell Aylmer?

He could worry about that later; first, he had to get away.

The dog was growling, deep in its throat; if it could have barked it could have brought the house down. Mannering actually stooped down to pat its head, then went to the door.

He opened it.

He heard someone coming down the stairs.

As Mannering opened the door, he put out the torch; so there was no light. He made no sound, and in that moment the dog was also silent. Whoever came down did not stop. He might not be coming into the office, might not have been disturbed, it could be a routine check.

Nonsense!

The footsteps drew nearer.

Mannering drew back into the room. He pulled the door to, but didn't latch it; a clicking latch would give all the warning the man wanted. The danger now was from the dog; it had gone strangely quiet, as if it had also heard someone else.

He yelped!

The door opened.

Mannering was behind it; the handle actually pushed into his padded stomach. Light flashed on, flooding the room, showing the huge Alsatian on the floor, the safe which looked untouched, the desk and drawing-board.

" Jumbo ! " Jeff Liddicombe cried, and darted towards the dog. He was wearing pyjamas, red and white stripes, and he looked huge. " What the hell——"

Mannering stepped from behind the door, for as easy a job as he was ever likely to have. He rapped Liddicombe on the back of the neck with the side of his hand, and as the innkeeper started up, arms raised convulsively,

Mannering took his right wrist and thrust his arm up and behind him in a hammerlock.

"Don't move, don't shout," he breathed.

Liddicombe tried desperately to turn round; but he couldn't see who it was. He back heeled, and Mannering jerked his arm up sharply; he gasped with the pain, and went still.

Mannering said: "Now we'll talk. Who'd you work for?"

Liddicombe was gasping for breath.

Mannering pushed the arm a fraction further. "*Who do you work for?*"

"Let go—my *arm*!"

"I'll break it if you don't answer. *Who d'you work for?*"

Liddicombe's breathing was coming in short, sharp gasps. The dog was whining while trying desperately to get out of its bonds. There was too much noise, and only seconds to spare.

"Come on, let's have it," Mannering rasped, "when I say I'll break——"

He didn't hear a sound behind him.

He just felt the terrific blow on the back of the head.

The blow didn't knock him out, but it knocked him silly. He let Liddicombe's arm go, staggered to one side, came up against the drawing-board and set it rocking. He steadied, but he didn't have time to save himself from another attack. He just saw the face of the man who was striking at him, and recognised one thing for certain; the cold, deliberate pleasure the man took in striking.

He still didn't lose consciousness.

The blows stopped.

Mannering leaned against the drawing-board, gasping for breath, feeling his cut lips, his bruised cheeks, one eye swelling rapidly. The savagery of the attack made it hard to realise that it had stopped. He could only see a blur, but gradually shapes sorted themselves out.

Liddicombe was on his knees, by the side of the dog. The other man was standing in the doorway, watching sardonically. He'd been in the bar, Mannering knew.

The cords fell to one side, and the dog got slowly to its feet.

" Want to feel its fangs ? " Liddicombe asked roughly. " Want them buried in your throat ? "

The white teeth were shiny, the dog's mouth was wide open with saliva dripping ; and it was straining to leap at Mannering:

" If you don't talk——" Liddicombe began but he didn't finish. The other man snatched the scarf off Mannering's face, and Liddicombe's mouth drooped in surprise. " *Richardson !* From——" he gulped.

" Richardson, is it ? " asked the other man softly. " What's he got in his mouth ? " He stretched out and hooked just a finger inside Mannering's mouth ; one of the cheek pads, dislodged by the blows, fell out. " Cheek pad," he said, as softly. " Tie that dog up and go and hold this guy, Lid."

Liddicombe said : " He doesn't want tying up. Stay there, Jumbo, guard him."

Mannering saw him let the dog go.

It looked as if nothing could stop it from leaping, it actually crouched back on all fours.

" *Guard him !* " Liddicombe cried.

The dog didn't leap.

Liddicombe went behind Mannering, grabbed him by the wrist, and thrust his arm up in the hammerlock.

It wasn't so much pain as despair which filled Mannering then.

The man who had struck him was of medium size, heavily built and pale-faced, moved with restrained roughness. He forced Mannering's mouth open, and hooked out the other pad ; then looked at his teeth. He took a bunch of keys from his pocket and scraped the teeth ; the plastic covering wrinkled. He worked this loose, and tore it away.

Staring, he said : " Permanganate, probably, the usual

stuff. We can soon rub that off. See anything familiar about him ? "

Liddicombe let Mannering go. The dog growled. Liddicombe stepped in front of Mannering, and stared. Then :

" No."

" Sure ? "

" Yes."

The other man laughed on a deep, satisfied note.

" You're slipping, Jeff ! Won't old Bony Face be pleased ? We've found Mr. Ruddy Mannering, and he won't get away. All we want now is the Woburn woman, and then Bony Face can do what he likes. I won't be sorry when it's over." He paused, lit a cigarette slowly, and puffed the smoke into Mannering's face with cruel insolence. " You're a worker, I'll say that for you," he said, " it's almost a pity you're on the other side. What did you come for ? "

Mannering said heavily : " For a plan of the roof of Brook House."

" What the hell made you come here for that ? " Liddicombe demanded.

" You're a good draughtsman, aren't you ? " Mannering said.

There was no point in refusing to answer, for obviously they daren't let him go. The attack had been so savage and fierce that he was still feeling the effect. The speed with which his assailant had spotted the disguise, once the cheek pad was loose, took hope away.

For those few minutes, he saw no hope at all.

" Told the police about this ? " Liddicombe snapped.

Mannering didn't answer. He just saw the possibility of worrying them, of lying, of making them think the police were after them.

The stranger said : " He wouldn't tell the police about a job like this, he wants the kudos. Famous amateur 'tec beats the cops ! " The gibe came sneeringly. " We don't have to worry about this. We've only got one thing to worry about—do we kill him now or do we try to use him to get the woman ? "

21

BAIT.

MANNERING TRIED NOT TO LOOK AT EITHER OF THEM ;
tried not to show his fear. He felt better now than
he had been a few seconds ago ; he would be better still
in five minutes, when he'd recovered from the shock.
They needn't *see* how much they had frightened him.

Liddicombe said : " How could we do that, Micky ? "

" That's our worry," said the man named Micky.
" We want the pair of them, don't we, and it isn't so
easy to get at anyone in Brook House, unless we persuade
your little Prissy to drop poison in the soup."

Liddicombe snapped : " That's out."

" Nothing's out if Seale gets really worked up," retorted
Micky smoothly. " But who'd want to see Priscilla in
trouble, Jeff ? We'll find another way." His grin was
very broad. " Maybe Priscilla could give the Woburn
woman a message."

Liddicombe didn't speak.

Mannering was thinking : " They'll postpone it, whatever else." The impending sense of death receded a little,
he could breathe. But he couldn't move. The dog still
crouched on its haunches, watching from unwinking eyes.

" What kind of message ? " the innkeeper asked at last.

" Maybe that Mannering wants to see her, maybe that
Mr. *Richardson* does," sneered Micky. " What do we
have to do ? Get her to drive——"

He broke off.

Liddicombe said : " We don't take any risks with
Priscilla, get that into your head."

" Okay, Jeff, okay ! But what's eating you ? This
is what we do. We have Prissy tell the Woburn woman
that *Merrow* wants to see her at the hospital. She'll go
running. And it's one that the police will bite, too.

We'll say that Richardson wants to talk to Merrow and Woburn at the hospital. So she'll drive. The police-car will follow her, as it always does, but why should that stop us? We'll get both the police-car and the girl on the road. Now we've got Mannering, we can afford to do that—there's only the one more chance to take. And afterwards——"

He broke off.

Liddicombe said: "So long as you leave my daughter out of it. She's done plenty."

"I'll say she's done plenty," Micky agreed, "and she'll get plenty out of it, won't she?"

Liddicombe didn't answer.

Micky said: "What do we do with Mannering?" He gave a bark of a laugh, of gloating delight. "We really got Mannering, he walked right into our hands! Tell you what, old Bony Face will be glad to lose some beauty sleep over this, I'll phone him and ask him what he says. Do we cut Mannering's throat now, or has he any questions to ask him?"

"You don't phone Bony Face from here, you can go into Orme in the morning and do that," Liddicombe said firmly. "One sentence for the exchange to pick up and we'd be for it. We can put Mannering in the cellar under the barn, he'll keep there." Liddicombe wasn't smiling; probably he still felt the effect of the shock. "We can't afford to make any mistakes, see? If you throw a grenade at the woman's car and get caught, the police will find out you've been staying here, and——"

"You're a hell of a sight jittery," Micky scoffed. "I was just staying near by, wasn't I? No one will tie you up with this now that we've found Mannering. He's nearly as good as they say he is!" He turned to Mannering, sneering, mocking. "You're going to have a nice long rest. And here's something to keep you company. If we want to get any information out of you, we'll use a pal of ours to help us. Won't we, Jumbo? You see that dog? Can you imagine anything he'd like more than to tear you to pieces. Eh, Jumbo?"

The dog growled.

"Okay," said Micky. He snatched a cushion from the easy chair, and thrust it into Mannering's face; Mannering, half suffocated, couldn't do a thing to save himself. They took the cushion away and tied a scarf roughly round his mouth, drawing it tightly enough to force his lips wide open; then they tied his hands behind his back. Next they led him out of the room, along a passage, to a flight of narrow stairs.

The smell of beer, unpleasant because it was so concentrated and stale, was heavy on the air. Mannering went down the stone steps, and in the cellar he had ample room to stand upright. Liddicombe was forcing him along, and they reached the wall at the far end. Passages within the cellar led right and left, with wine bins on either side.

The wall at the end seemed blank.

Micky stretched up, and pulled at one of the bricks just above his head. It moved. He pulled again, and a part of the wall moved silently on oiled hinges. Beyond it was pitch dark.

There was a scuffling sound of rats.

"We'll leave Jumbo outside to make sure that Mannering doesn't get a chance," Micky said. "Don't mind having your breakfast down here, Jumbo, do you?"

The dog growled.

"In he goes," Micky said.

Liddicombe gave Mannering a push. He stumbled against the bricks at the foot of the doorway, and couldn't save himself. The side of the 'door' saved him. He stepped through, into the darkness—and one of the men pushed him off his balance.

He fell, helplessly, twisting his body to save his face. He hit the floor with his shoulder and temple, and lay half stunned.

When he began to come round, it was pitch dark.

They had taken his tools; his gun; nearly everything from his pockets. This was a cellar, and almost certainly had only one entry; the walled-up entry which no one knew about. Outside, the Alsatian would be on guard, and there was nothing the dog would like more than to savage him.

Mannering lay there for long, helpless minutes.

Then he began to pick himself up; with his arms tied behind him, it wasn't easy. A few minutes in the darkness told him how utterly black it was; Stygian gloom, if ever he had known it. He moved cautiously until he kicked against a wall. Although he had headed for one, it caught him by surprise; he banged his knee and his nose.

"Damn!" he exclaimed.

He leaned against the wall. He felt very weak, his face was painful, his right eye still swelling and feeling tight. His nose stung. His ears were filled with buzzing noises. He knew that there was not the slightest chance of either of these men relenting; he had only a few hours to live, if they had their way. He knew that they could kill Joanna Woburn, and giving her a message from Merrow was the certain way to lure her from the house.

The police might check, to make sure that the message was genuine; if they didn't——

All this, and the best he could manage was "*Damn!*"

He giggled.

Across the giggling came the realisation that he was very near the point of despair, and that hysteria had been born out of it. The prospect of escape was as black as the darkness of the cellar, but the quick way to death was the way of despair. He might die; he could at least *try* to find a way out; to get a warning to Joanna; to tell the police.

Above him, the men were back in their rooms.

Outside the door, the dog lay with its nose between its paws, staring at the brickwork of the door.

Mannering began to move about the cellar, keeping his shoulder against the wall to make sure that he didn't get away from the wall and begin to move in circles.

At Brook House, Joanna Woburn woke a little after seven o'clock, and lay still, realising that something was unusual, unfamiliar—and welcome. Then she realised it was the simple fact that she had no headache. She relaxed, revelling in that sense of freedom. For several days she had felt all the time as if her head would burst; now, there was hope that she was over the effects of the shock.

She looked at a bedside clock; it was half-past seven.

Five minutes afterwards she got up and went to the window. There was a mist over the parkland, which suggested that it would be warm later on. She saw one of the maids running along the vegetable garden, and that reminded her of Priscilla and of George. It didn't hurt as it had done, something had eased the burden.

Perhaps things would get better from now on.

She rang the bell for tea. Mrs. Baddelow brought it, full of plaints. Priscilla had gone to the 'Grey Mare', her father had been taken ill, or some such nonsense, just at the busiest time of the day they were a maid short; Mrs. Baddelow talked as if that were a major tragedy.

"And such a nice *morning*," she said bitterly.

Joanna was glad when she had gone.

She sat in an easy chair looking out of the window, and knowing that Orme, the hospital and George were straight across country from here. It was good to be able to think about George Merrow without hurt. She found herself dwelling on all the things he had said, on his talk of being in love with her.

She knew one thing for certain: she was in love with him.

At eight, she bathed.

At nine, she was having breakfast.

At half-past, Priscilla came somewhat diffidently into the dining-room. Priscilla could be demure, timid or truculent; this was her timid mood; in fact she was almost nervous. The sun shone on her hair and Joanna found herself thinking:

"She's really quite lovely. With the proper make-up and good clothes——"

She made herself smile.

"Good-morning, Priscilla. I hope your father isn't too bad."

"Oh, it's a false alarm, always getting the wind up about his health," said Priscilla off-handedly. "I—er—I went into Orme to get some medicine for him, miss, Mrs. Baddelow said I could. And I—er—looked in to see Mr. Merrow."

Joanna felt herself stiffening.

"Oh, did you?"

"Yes, miss. He—he asked me to give you a message, miss!" Joanna's heart leapt; and the girl went on as if she couldn't speak slowly any longer. "Yes, miss, he wondered if you could look in and see him this morning, about half-past ten, he said he had something important he wanted to say to you."

Joanna hated herself for colouring so furiously.

"Thank you, Priscilla. I'll try to arrange it."

"I know he'll be ever so pleased, miss," Priscilla said.

Joanna went to speak to White.

As soon as Joanna Woburn had left him, White telephoned Aylmer; he didn't have long to wait. He didn't have a chance to suggest that the maid's story be checked, either; for Joanna had simply said that she was going in to see Merrow.

"Leaving here at ten o'clock," White said. "I'll have her followed, sir, if you'll have everything laid on to watch her when she gets in the town among the crowd. That's the danger spot, I'd say."

"I'll lay it on," promised Aylmer. "Any bright ideas from the private dick?"

"Still asleep," White said, and chuckled. "Got a 'don't disturb' card hanging on his door, he must have been celebrating deep into the night!"

They both laughed.

"Ten o'clock," thought Joanna. "Ten minutes—oh, what a fool I am!"

She laughed at herself.

She felt a sense of gaiety, because she felt sure that George wanted to see her. Whatever he'd done in the past, whatever the truth about the women in his life, it could all be worked out; it must be.

She went out into the grounds, and strolled towards the garage.

Micky was waiting near a blind corner hidden from the road by the wall of a bridge which spanned the little stream. It was a perfect spot. He could see through a gap in a hedge all the traffic heading from Orme come into his line of vision.

He was thinking how pleased Seale had sounded on the telephone; and how pleased and relieved Greer had sounded, too.

The hand-grenades—he had two—were too heavy for his pocket. He put them on the ground, making a dent with his heel so that they couldn't roll away. Near him, the river gurgled and the birds, no longer curious or scared, flew about as if he were part of the countryside.

The girl was to be killed first; then Mannering.

Again Mannering said wearily: " *Damn !* "

He caught his side against something in the wall, on the third time round. It hurt. He must have been pressing closer than he had on the first two walks. He was at a stage when the idea that he must try to get out was fading, because it was so obviously impossible. It was hot, and he was drooping already. He had not realised how badly he had been battered.

So, he damned the 'thing'.

He went on.

He stopped, and his heart gave a curious little leap, the kind that meant that he was feeling alive again. He made his way back very carefully, until he touched the 'thing', which pressed into his side. He went past it, feeling it catch in his coat. He explored very cautiously with his hands, and at last stood so that he could touch the 'thing', which was cold, as metal would be.

It was a big nail.

He was hardly breathing when he discovered it, and
when he tried to stand so that the head of the nail caught
in the cord round his wrists. He tugged ; and the cord
slipped off. That was it, that was exactly what he
wanted ; friction. He worked until the cord was over
the head of the nail again, then began to saw gently to
and fro. The strain on his arms in the unaccustomed
position brought pain and cramp sooner than he expected
The worst was just above the elbows, near the biceps.
He rested, sawed, rested, sawed. He couldn't be sure
whether he was making any progress, could only hope.
He wouldn't let himself tug, until he really thought there
was a hope.

He tugged, putting all his strength into the effort.

The cord held.

He sawed and rested, sawed and rested, sawed.

He tugged, and it broke.

Now, he felt almost stifled. For a few seconds he
could only lean against the wall, fighting against physical
weakness. It eased. He straightened up, and began to
work his arms about, then to rub his wrists. He hadn't
been tied up long enough for the circulation to be seriously
affected ; he had pins and needles, that was all.

He worked the scarf off, and moved his mouth to ease
the pain but he wasn't thinking about pain.

Had they left him *anything* ?

Could he get that nail out of the wall, and use it ?

He groped in his pockets. Cigarettes—lighter ! He
was so parched that it did not even occur to him to
smoke. Very funny. Cigarettes, lighter, money, but
no tools. At least, he had a light. It was surprising
how quickly one became used to the darkness.

He flicked the lighter.

The nail was so far inside the wall that he knew there
wasn't a ghost of a chance of levering it out ; so that
hope was gone. He felt his teeth clenching as he looked
round as far as the light would carry. In one corner
was a pile of shavings, and several old sacks. There were

dozens of empty wine bottles, too, but no casks with metal hasps he might use as a tool; nothing that would help him to prise bricks away.

He looked up at the ceiling. The plaster was flaking and here and there it had come away, showing the gap between the laths which held it, and the floor boards of the old barn. The Museum; they had said that this cellar was beneath that, hadn't they?

He saw a crack of light.

He stared, hands and teeth clenching in unison. It wasn't imagination, there was a tiny crack of daylight where the boards didn't join properly.

Could he make use of it?

Could he break the ceiling down more, and push one of the boards up? One board would be almost enough, two would be plenty.

He looked at his watch. It was nearly half-past eight. Joanna wouldn't go into Orme yet, would she? Ten or eleven o'clock, more likely.

He had time.

He had to try to get up into the barn.

By standing on tiptoe, and pulling at the plaster with his fingers, he managed to get some of it down. Chippings and dust fell into his eyes; they watered badly and began to smart, but he didn't stop.

At the end of a quarter of an hour he had cleared a hole in the plaster nearly an inch square; an inch.

It would take hours to reach the boards.

22

START OF A JOURNEY

JOANNA PRESSED THE SELF-STARTER. THE ENGINE turned at the first touch, whirred, and then faded out. She pressed three times before it roared as if it meant to keep going. The car was facing the drive; she had only to drive out, and go straight down, turn right into Orme Hill where she would pass the 'Grey Mare', three miles on across the bridge, and then she would have a straight run into Orme itself.

She tried to picture George Merrow's face.

It wasn't easy; somehow, the mind picture kept clouding. All she could see clearly was his twisted, almost cruel expression whenever he talked so bitterly. Cruel? She sensed that he had been desperately hurt, and knew that she owed much of her new understanding to Richardson.

Where *was* Richardson?

Joanna looked up at her own window, then at his. It was open a little at the top, as it had been ever since he had come here. In her line of vision was the top of the chimney stack.

She drove slowly down the drive for a while, to give the police escort good time. She was in a desperate hurry, and yet felt that she wanted to take her time. She didn't want to rush carelessly into the ward. She even allowed herself the fear that he did not want her to tell her why he had behaved so strangely, why he talked of love and then rebuffed her.

She wondered why Richardson hadn't been down to breakfast, and then put thought of him out of her mind. The police-car was giving trouble. She was content to sit and wait for a few minutes, but soon grew restive; she hoped that it wouldn't take much longer to get the police-car's engine going.

It started.

It was twenty minutes past ten.

Mannering stared at the tiny hole in the plaster, and the crack between the boards, the only one he could see. There must be a slight fault in one of the boards, so that it had cracked. No other sliver of light appeared.

He had no tool with which to push the boards up.

He had no way of attracting attention——

Hadn't he ?

He could start a fire, because they had left him his lighter !

The thought came storming his mind, and he thrust it away ; it came again so that he had to look at it squarely. *He could start a fire.* He could burn the shavings and the old sacks, and possibly the wooden floor would catch. If it did, and no one realised that he was underneath——

He shut the thought out.

He considered it again.

Joanna would be going in to see Merrow. He did not doubt that Priscilla had done what her father had ordered, and that the message had been delivered. She might now be on the way. She might now be dead, but—it was only twenty minutes past nine. He still doubted whether she would start so early. He knew that he was only guessing, but he had to guess, and—he had to attract attention.

The only chance was by starting the fire.

He gathered the bottles together, laying down two rows of ten each, nine on the ten ; eight on the nine. He built them up to a peak, making every move swift and decisive, now that he had taken the decision. He forgot pain, tiredness and fear. He touched the neck of a bottle and it fell, bringing others down with it. He built the pyramid up again, and when he was satisfied, rested some shavings on top of it and old sacks on that.

Would the heat of the fire make the bottles collapse ?

He flicked his lighter, hesitated for a moment with the

flame close to the shavings, and then slowly placed it under them. The wood flared, then died down; the lighter wick kept burning. He started again, and this time the shavings caught properly, but not fiercely. Belatedly he poked some shavings in between the plaster and the barn floor, and lit them; they burned only sluggishly.

He went round to the other side, and started the main fire there. Now flame shot upwards, hissing with the resin in the dry wood. The sacking began to smoulder, and the smell of burning became pungent.

Mannering stood watching.

Once it was burning well, it would be difficult to put out; perhaps impossible. He felt the heat, and the first promise of what it could do. A spark flew, and stung him on the back of the head. He backed away a yard. Now the shavings were burning fiercely and the sacking doing what he had meant it to—smouldering. Smoke poured up, grey and powerful-smelling, struck the top of the ceiling and hid the hole in the plaster. Then it spread out on the ceiling, and coiled down on Mannering's head.

He lay on the floor—and started to cough.

It was very hot.

This was only a small cellar, and wouldn't take long to fill. He had a pencil, and they'd left him his wallet; he took out a Quinns card, and wrote: "Liddicombe and man named Micky plan to hold up and kill Joanna Woburn this morning." It was enough for the police, if, when they found him, he wasn't able to talk. He held it lightly. Then he jerked his head up, sharply, as understanding came. He added in swift, sharp strokes: "Check death of a man named Holden, September ten years ago. Check identity of——" He dropped the card in another fit of coughing, picked it up, but couldn't write any more. The worst part was that he could do nothing, except get as far away as possible from the burning, and watch; and choke. The bouts of coughing came more frequently, he could hardly pause between them. They hurt his head, his face and his stomach, now; he fought to keep still, but paroxysms took him and shook him.

His eyes were stinging.

The smoke was coiling and writhing, and he could only just see the glow in the middle. He didn't know whether any was escaping through that tiny slit, but suddenly he felt that it was a waste of effort, that he had thrown his life away.

Very little would escape through that slit, so little that unless someone stepped into the barn, they probably wouldn't see the smoke. Only the hostelry's staff were likely to enter during the morning; most likely Liddicombe himself. Liddicombe might even make sure that no one else visited it.

The stench and the heat of burning were heavy in his nostrils. The cloying thickness of the smoke was in his mouth, his nose, in the back of his throat. His breathing came in short, sharp gusts. He didn't know whether the smoke was getting thicker or not. His heart hammered and his head whirled, as if it wanted to keep time with the writhing smoke. He couldn't see the glow. He was aware only of the heat, the thick air, the air which crawled into his lungs like something thick and foul, something which blocked all the air passages, and which wouldn't let him breathe in the sweet air that they wanted.

His head was numbed, now.

His limbs felt light.

He kept coughing, and was weaker after every bout. He was conscious of the awful burden of failure; of the approach of death for himself and for Joanna Woburn.

He thought of Lorna.

It had been just a casual job; not even a commission. Jimmy Garfield hadn't done any business with him for years. The old man had sent that S O S and Mannering had gone hurrying; if he hadn't been suspicious about what might happen to Joanna on the road, he would have stayed completely free from trouble.

Well, he hadn't.

He was coughing spasmodically, but it no longer hurt. Nothing hurt. He knew that he was losing consciousness, and strangely enough, it didn't matter. Funny way to go out. All his life he had been fighting, often he had lived by violence, more often than not he had lived dangerously. It wouldn't have been so bad had he been able to fight now. He *could* fight! He put the card beneath him, safe from burning, certain to be discovered.

Certain?

The smoke was filling his lungs, and suffocating him. He coughed, drearily.

The smoke was thicker, the fire glowed very red, the heat would have been unbearable if he had been conscious; as it was, he was hardly aware of it.

He didn't hear the crash when part of the ceiling fell in, or hear the roar of the flames as they shot up into the old barn.

It was half-past ten.

Joanna saw the smoke soon after she turned the corner from the drive. She didn't know exactly where it was, but it seemed to be somewhere near the ' Grey Mare '. She heard the engine of the police-car rev up, and the driver waved her down as he shot past her, to investigate. She slowed down. It could be a crashed car on fire. It could be another attack, or a form of attack.

She had to turn two corners before reaching the bend in the road which showed her exactly where the fire was. Smoke was pouring out of the Old Barn, where two or three men were standing about helplessly, two with pails of water. One man was bellowing, and a dog was barking; she knew Jeff Liddicombe's Alsatian and recognised its deep, baying note.

The police-car had stopped, and the driver came back.

" Better wait for a bit, Miss Woburn." He smiled. " Sorry. Fire-brigade will be here in a minute, don't want to run into trouble with it on those bends. Safer this side of the smoke, anyhow."

"I must get into Orme——"

"Won't keep you a minute longer than we must, miss."

There was nothing she could say about that, she could only watch the smoke. It was getting thicker, and she thought that she saw a red glow, as if the old timbers of the barn had caught fire.

"One good thing, no one'd be in there," the policeman said. "Only trouble will be if the wind changes. Going straight across the road at the moment, though."

"Look!" Joanna exclaimed. "It's getting fiercer."

It was glowing bright red, and now they could hear the flames. The smell of smoke was wafted back. She stood by the side of the police-car, thoughts of Merrow pushed aside by the sight of the rolling smoke and glowing fire.

Liddicombe had the big dog by the leash, but was having great difficulty in holding him; for once, he couldn't be controlled. The men with the buckets of water had given up the unequal fight, and were standing and watching.

Then the fire-bell clanged, and the red engine loomed out of the smoke. It drew to one side, and helmeted men jumped off. Joanna was fascinated by the speed with which they set to work. She saw three smash their way into the Old Barn, and others follow; none came out. Hoses was rushed to a nearby hydrant and jets of water poured on the outhouses of the 'Grey Mare'.

Then the dog broke away from Liddicombe, and disappeared, terrified by the flames. Liddicombe stood with his hands raised heavenwards, as if in supplication.

Soon, two helmeted firemen went inside the Old Barn.

The floor had caved in, by one wall. Through the hole, the men could see what looked like the body of a man.

Ten minutes later, Joanna saw the body of a man being brought out of the barn. She went forward, trying to see who it was. Then a car pulled up at the inn for a moment, and the driver spoke to a fireman.

"That's the Guv'nor's car," the police-driver exclaimed.

"You mean Superintendent Aylmer's?"

"Yes."

Aylmer, with a man by his side, started off again, driving as if the furies were after him. He was peering hard at Joanna and, twenty yards away, he jammed on his brakes. The car actually skidded into the hedge. Joanna turned to look at him, the policeman hurried forward, and Aylmer came running.

"*You all right, Miss Woburn?*"

Of course she was all right, couldn't he see?

He was gasping for breath.

"Yes," she said.

"Thank God for that. Just found Mannering. In the cellar." Aylmer gulped. "He's unconscious but—there's a written note which says Liddicombe had planned to kill you this morning. We've got Liddicombe, but another of the devils is still at large. So is Liddicombe's daughter, Priscilla. She might be as deadly as——"

He broke off.

Priscilla Liddicombe, on a bicycle, turned a corner in the road and came tearing towards them.

23

A QUESTION OF IDENTITY

AYLMER AND THE OTHER DETECTIVE STOOD TOGETHER in front of Joanna, as if to shield her from attack; and Priscilla looked as if she were ready to attack. She put every ounce of strength into her movements, and as she drew nearer, her eyes glistened as if she were filled with murderous intent. At sight of Aylmer, she stopped pedalling and jammed on the brakes; for a moment it looked as if she would be tossed over the handlebars. Aylmer ducked.

She steadied herself, and sprang off the machine.

"Now, young woman——" Aylmer began.

"Never mind the talk," Priscilla Liddicombe gasped. "There's a man waiting to—to blow Miss Woburn into little pieces! He's hiding by a bridge. Don't ask me how I know, I don't have to talk, but that's the size of it. Chap named Micky. And that man Richardson's some-where—somewhere in the 'Grey Mare'." She gulped. "I don't know where, I don't know anything else about it!"

"Where is this Micky?" Aylmer demanded sharply.

"*Some*where! I don't know any more, I just had to tell you, I——"

Priscilla broke off, staring towards the inn; it was obvious that she only realised what the smoke meant at that moment.

"It's *burning*," she breathed. "Richardson might be there, in the cellar."

Aylmer said with a wincing note in his voice: "It's the old barn that's on fire. You're dead right. Richardson was there; whether he'll come round or not I don't know".

The girl swayed. Joanna moved, to hold her; and stood with her arms round her shoulders. Aylmer stared at the smoke and the man on the stretcher.

A man came up, with a card, and said something about finding it beneath Mannering. Aylmer was soon calling orders. Joanna saw him drive off; another police-car followed. She went towards the inert figure which had been brought from the cellar.

Richardson?

No, it wasn't; anyhow, he looked different.

John *Mannering*!

She watched them put him in an ambulance, which had just arrived, and she did not know whether he was alive.

Aylmer and two policemen approached the bridge from the fields and thickets behind it, and took Micky by surprise. He did grab one of the grenades, but Aylmer wrested it from him and hurled it into the river. Its explosion terrified a thousand birds and as many rabbits, but did no harm.

Bristow got out of his car near Hampstead Heath, and talked to a detective-inspector from the local division. They were not within sight of Seale's house, but it was surrounded at a distance, and watched from the windows of neighbouring houses. Anyone who left there would be detained; but no one left. Bristow knew what had happened in Orme Hill; knew that it was touch and go with Mannering. He felt a savage eagerness to raid the house and to hold Seale and Greer, whom Liddicombe had named; but he knew that if they staged a raid, the men inside would shoot it out.

They might not know what had happened.

So Bristow moved from one of the loosely flung cordon to another. All he knew about Seale and Greer fitted in with what had happened.

A man came hurrying.

" Mr. Bristow, sir."

" Yes? " Bristow turned his back on the green of the heath, the trees, the brambles where Wilberforce had been murdered.

" Door's open, sir, and three men and a woman are getting in a car. Any instructions? "

"So they're on the run," Bristow said, and his eyes showed deep satisfaction. "All right, we'll lay on a reception." He flashed messages by walkie-talkie to the other police-cars, and they made their way towards the ends of the street where Seale lived. Bristow was at one corner when he saw the car coming out. It was a roomy Austin, and doubtless had a nice turn of speed. Greer was at the wheel, Seale beside him, a man and a woman with a lot of corn-coloured hair were in the back seats. Bristow drove along as if he weren't interested in them. He sensed Seale's gaze. He didn't know whether Seale or the others would recognise him.

If Seale had a gun——

They were almost alongside, the Austin gathering speed, when Bristow wrenched his wheel. The two cars met sideways on, and the Austin swayed. Greer trod on the accelerator, the engine roared, the cars scraped noisily—and the bumpers locked.

The Austin's engine stalled.

Seale, his face more than ever like a robot's, raised a gun and pointed at Bristow through the open window. Bristow ducked desperately, but knew that he hadn't a chance if the man fired.

Then a second police-car banged into the back of the Austin, the bullet smashed the windscreen and did no harm; police rushed the cars before Seale or Greer or the others had a chance.

Bristow watched them being led away.

It was all over bar the shouting, he knew; the shouting, and the waiting to find out what happened to Mannering.

Mannering lived.

But before the day was out, Jimmy Garfield had a sharp relapse, and died.

Joanna was at the hospital with Merrow when that happened.

Five days later, looking exactly like himself and feeling almost fit, Mannering walked down the great staircase at Brook House. He felt as light-hearted as he had for a long, long time.

He had spent an hour with Lorna the previous evening, and there was no longer the slightest danger for her. He knew that George Merrow was back at the house, confined to his bed but making good progress. He knew of the odd friendship which had now developed between Priscilla Liddicombe and Joanna Woburn. Joanna's chief fear appeared to be that the police would level some charge against Priscilla.

Mannering did not think they would.

The girl had been under her father's orders, and terrified of him. She had spied on the occupants of Brook House, and reported every move. She had also admitted Liddicombe to the house so that he had been able to go up to the roof and make the plan for the burglary.

She had fallen in love with George Merrow, too.

Then, after her father's orders on the morning that had seen the end of it all, she had obeyed precisely, and told Joanna the lie. She would probably never be able to explain her frame of mind during that hour or two; how she had been torn between fear of her father, and dread of what might happen to other people. She had always known that Liddicombe was a man of violence, but tried to shut her mind to it. She had not been told directly of the plot to kill Joanna, but remarks made by Micky and her father had made their purpose clear. She had brooded over them, knowing exactly where Micky was waiting.

She had believed that she had a chance of winning George Merrow without Joanna; so she had watched Joanna drive off, for those few minutes had wanted her to die. Then something had cracked inside her, she had realised the full horror of what she was doing. In sudden desperation she had taken the cycle and ridden over the grassland, taking paths which gave her a chance to head Joanna off.

Mannering was pondering over this as he went into the library.

Aylmer and Bristow were already there, Bristow looking relaxed and comparatively cheerful. Two local detectives were also present. George Merrow was wheeled in, with Joanna behind the wheel-chair, looking like a princess out of Scandinavian legends. It was easy to forget Merrow's expression because of his startling good looks.

" Well, what's the dictatorial summons about ? " Merrow demanded. " Who's done what wrong now ? "

Mannering chuckled.

Bristow said : " Mr. Mannering seems to think he has a useful contribution to make to our general knowledge, Mr. Merrow, and we would like you here for confirmation of certain parts of his statement."

Merrow shrugged. " Maybe this is the confirmation you want." He took a sealed envelope from his pocket and held it out. " A signed statement which should persuade you to keep the dogs off me."

Bristow took it. " Thanks." He didn't open it. " Be interesting to see how right you are, Mannering."

Mannering said mildly : " Nice of you, Bill. I'm not going to keep you long, though. It concerns the contents of the black box, of course, which we were told were miniatures. Nothing of the kind, as you now know—but you have the box and contents, I haven't seen it. I'm just guessing."

Bristow snorted.

" Fact," said Mannering brightly. " That box did contain a kind of miniature, I've no doubt at all. Miniature documents—tiny photostat copies of evidence to send Seale, Liddicombe and the others of the mob to jail, perhaps to the gallows. Right ? "

Bristow exclaimed : " And you *guessed* that ? Not on your life. You must have known all along."

" That's the trouble with policemen, they have no faith in human nature or perceptiveness," Mannering said. " I didn't know, Bill. But it had to be something that Seale would kill to get ; something which could be effective after Jimmy Garfield's death, in the right hands.

Something, I think, he wanted to get to me, hoping I'd tackle Seale and company. I think he was going to confide in me, and hope I'd help him without confiding in you."

Bristow growled: "That's right. There was a letter in the box, saying just that. He'd meant Merrow to bring it to you, and when Merrow was injured, put it on to Miss Woburn."

"Confide in you about what?" asked Joanna slowly.

Bristow said: "Go on, Oracle."

Mannering chuckled.

"Recognition at last!" He didn't continue at once, and in fact his smile faded; he looked serious, almost diffident. "Jimmy *wasn't* the real Garfield," he said quietly. "The genuine J. G. had died. The Jimmy who lived here impersonated him. Seale knew that, and tried to blackmail Jimmy. Jimmy countered with those photostat copies. Checkmate."

He paused.

Joanna, a hand on Merrow's shoulder, said in a hushed voice:

"Oh, no."

"Oh, yes," Merrow said. He gripped her hand. "Jimmy told me about it. That's why I kept quiet. I've put it all in the statement."

There was silence, and Bristow broke it quietly, almost reluctantly.

"No doubt it's true, Miss Woburn. The man you knew as Garfield was really a man named Holden. The real Garfield died a natural death. He had few friends, and Holden seized a chance to succeed in one of the boldest impersonation frauds in history." Bristow gulped, as if he hated to admit that, but didn't pause for long. "Just before his death, the real Garfield had bought this house. He died intestate, and Holden, your Jimmy, took over—according to a letter he kept at his bank to be opened after his death, he thought he was only cheating the State. Then afterwards he discovered an heir—a nephew whom the real Garfield had cut off because of some quarrel. Jimmy sent for Merrow, paid his fare, told him the truth. Merrow took to the old man, and was prepared to wait for his inheritance, and not give Jimmy away.

"All the time, your Jimmy dealt by letter, telephone and through agents when he took over. He was a brilliant forger, and a serious accident—the one which paralysed him—had altered his appearance a great deal. He had only to keep from people who knew him well, to get away with the impersonation. There was one exception—Gedde, who was an old friend of Jimmy's. With Gedde as a conspirator, the impersonation had its big chance of success.

"It worked perfectly—until, in the last few years, Jimmy had this fight with Seale on his hands.

"Seale wanted to take over the house, the fortune, the treasures kept here; to come into the open, live his life here freely. So, as a blackmailer and killer, he had to keep in the background.

"He hated Jimmy.

"He bore a grudge which turned him from an ordinary crook into a cold-blooded killer. You won't want more details about him, what's happened speaks for itself, but——"

He paused again.

Merrow said: "There are things we do want made clear, Mr. Bristow. That Jimmy wasn't a killer. He spent a fortune seeking me out—seeking the real Garfield's nephew, remember, so that I should inherit.

"I wasn't much good, but—I liked Jimmy. He was a man in a million, crook or not. Soon after I got here, I realised that there was a lot of trouble. Jimmy told me what it was. He also told me that he was going to ask Mannering to help."

"What I didn't realise was that he wanted help for you, and was afraid you'd be killed," Mannering said.

"He wasn't scared for himself," Merrow agreed. He paused, then went on abruptly: "I was pretty sure there was a spy in the household. I checked the servants closely, and came to the conclusion that Priscilla was most likely." He looked up at Joanna, scowling. " And she was. Believe it or not, I set my cap at sweet Prissy, because I wanted to get the truth. That's the simple answer."

Joanna said chokily : " If only you'd told me——" She was staring down at Merrow as if she couldn't believe her ears.

" Never mind the means, I wanted to justify the end," Merrow said. " I hadn't much time for finer feelings, either. I felt that women owed me a lot that they'd never pay back. Priscilla would have talked, sooner or later. Once they actually fired at us when we were together, to scare Prissy into silence, and to scare me. They did ! "

" There isn't much more," Bristow put in unexpectedly. " Too much quixotism was the chief trouble." But he smiled at Merrow. " It was the decision to send for Mannering that brought matters to a head. Priscilla heard Jimmy and Merrow talking of that, and told her father. Seale made one last effort to get the photostats, so that he could take over. Priscilla Liddicombe let the man Pete in, to search for them. It didn't work out. Pete was seen by Garfield and Gedde. He hit him savagely, shot Gedde dead, and escaped. We know what happened after that."

Bristow waited.

" We know pretty well everything now, don't we ? " Mannering said. " Can you fill in the gaps, Bill ? "

Aylmer chuckled.

" *Very* funny," Bristow said dryly. " Well, I can try. Some of the bits and pieces fit in nicely. For instance, the old quarrel between Seale and Jimmy. They once swindled a kid who killed himself. Afterwards, Seale wanted to become a fence, Jimmy turned it down and turned Seale in. Seale tried to escape, stole a car, and was badly smashed up. His face is just one big job of plastic surgery ; he has other bone trouble which some-times makes it difficult for him to move freely. That's why he looks——" Bristow didn't finish, but asked abruptly. "Anything else worrying any of you?"

"Now that I'm through all this," said George Merrow, "I doubt if anything will ever worry me again."

His hand closed over Joanna's.

A few months later, after the trials and the executions, when all was calm again at Brook House and Orme, Joanna and George Merrow were married. Mannering and Lorna, Aylmer and Bristow and others associated with the case in which the Baron went into hiding, attended the wedding at the village church and the reception which would have done Jimmy Garfield proud.

There was a telegram of good wishes, signed 'Priscilla'.

"Where is she now?" Bristow asked.

"Got a job as an artist's model, in Chelsea," Aylmer said. "Mannering fixed it, didn't you, Mannering?"

"Blame or praise my wife," said Mannering. He looked at Lorna, who was watching Joanna and the bridegroom in the way that only women can; appraising and assessing. Lorna was calm and completely herself; it was hard to believe she had ever been close to death.

"What's that?" she asked absently, and before waiting for an answer, she went on: "Oh, they'll be happy—you don't need to ask!"

She wondered why Mannering laughed.

THE END

*If you have enjoyed this book, you might
wish to join the Walker British Mystery Society.*

*For information, please send a postcard or
letter to:*

Paperback Mystery Editor

**Walker & Company
720 Fifth Avenue
New York, NY 10019**